VOICES FROM THE RADIUM AGE

The Radium Age Book Series
Joshua Glenn

Voices from the Radium Age, edited by Joshua Glenn, 2022
A World of Women, J. D. Beresford, 2022
The World Set Free, H. G. Wells, 2022
The Clockwork Man, E. V. Odle, 2022

VOICES FROM THE RADIUM AGE

edited & introduced by
Joshua Glenn

THE MIT PRESS
CAMBRIDGE, MASSACHUSETTS
LONDON, ENGLAND

This book was set in Arnhem Pro and PF DIN Text Pro by New Best-set Typesetters Ltd. Printed and bound in the United States of America.

Library of Congress Cataloging-in-Publication Data

Names: Glenn, Joshua, 1967– editor.
Title: Voices from the radium age / edited by Joshua Glenn.
Description: Cambridge, Massachusetts : The MIT Press, [2022] | Series: The Radium Age series
Identifiers: LCCN 2021010590 | ISBN 9780262543378 (paperback)
Subjects: LCSH: Science fiction—20th century.
Classification: LCC PN6071.S33 V58 2022 | DDC 808.83/8762—dc23
LC record available at https://lccn.loc.gov/2021010590

10 9 8 7 6 5 4 3 2 1

CONTENTS

Series Foreword vii
Introduction xiii
Joshua Glenn

Sultana's Dream (1905) 1
Rokeya Sakhawat Hossain

The Voice in the Night (1907) 17
William Hope Hodgson

The Machine Stops (1909) 35
E. M. Forster

The Horror of the Heights (1913) 81
Arthur Conan Doyle

The Red One (1918) 105
Jack London

The Comet (1920) 141
W. E. B. Du Bois

The Jameson Satellite (1931) 161
Neil R. Jones

SERIES FOREWORD

Joshua Glenn

Do we really know science fiction? There were the scientific romance years that stretched from the mid-nineteenth century to circa 1900. And there was the genre's so-called golden age, from circa 1935 through the early 1960s. But between those periods, and overshadowed by them, was an era that has bequeathed us such tropes as the robot (berserk or benevolent), the tyrannical superman, the dystopia, the unfathomable extraterrestrial, the sinister telepath, and the eco-catastrophe. A dozen years ago, writing for the sf blog io9.com at the invitation of Annalee Newitz and Charlie Jane Anders, I became fascinated with the period during which the sf genre as we know it emerged. Inspired by the exactly contemporaneous career of Marie Curie, who shared a Nobel Prize for her discovery of radium in 1903, only to die of radiation-induced leukemia in 1934, I eventually dubbed this three-decade interregnum the "Radium Age."

Curie's development of the theory of radioactivity, which led to the extraordinary, terrifying, awe-inspiring insight that the atom is, at least in part, a state of energy constantly in movement, is an apt metaphor for the twentieth century's first three decades. These years were marked by rising sociocultural strife across various fronts: the founding of the women's suffrage movement, the National Association for the Advancement of Colored People, socialist currents within the labor movement, anticolonial and revolutionary upheaval around the world . . . as well as the associated strengthening of reactionary movements that supported, for example, racial segregation, immigration restriction, eugenics, and sexist policies.

Science—as a system of knowledge, a mode of experimenting, and a method of reasoning—accelerated the pace of change during these years in ways simultaneously liberating and terrifying. As sf author and historian Brian Stableford points out in his 1989 essay "The Plausibility of the Impossible," the universe we discovered by means of the scientific method in the early twentieth century defies common sense: "We are haunted by a sense of the impossibility of ultimately making sense of things." By playing host to certain far-out notions—time travel, faster-than-light travel, and ESP, for example—that we have every reason to judge impossible, science fiction serves as an "instrument of negotiation," Stableford suggests, with which we strive to accomplish "the difficult diplomacy of existence in a scientifically knowable but essentially unimaginable world." This is no less true today than during the Radium Age.

The social, cultural, political, and technological upheavals of the 1900–1935 period are reflected in the proto-sf writings of authors such as Olaf Stapledon, William Hope Hodgson, Muriel Jaeger, Karel Čapek, G. K. Chesterton, Cicely Hamilton, W. E. B. Du Bois, Yevgeny Zamyatin, E. V. Odle, Arthur Conan Doyle, Mikhail

Bulgakov, Pauline Hopkins, Stanisław Ignacy Witkiewicz, Aldous Huxley, Gustave Le Rouge, A. Merritt, Rudyard Kipling, Rose Macaulay, J. D. Beresford, J. J. Connington, S. Fowler Wright, Jack London, Thea von Harbou, and Edgar Rice Burroughs, not to mention the late-period but still incredibly prolific H. G. Wells himself. More cynical than its Victorian precursor yet less hard-boiled than the sf that followed, in the writings of these visionaries we find acerbic social commentary, shock tactics, and also a sense of frustrated idealism—and reactionary cynicism, too—regarding humankind's trajectory.

The MIT Press's Radium Age series represents a much-needed evolution of my own efforts to champion the best proto-sf novels and stories from 1900 to 1935 among scholars already engaged in the fields of utopian and speculative fiction studies, as well as general readers interested in science, technology, history, and thrills and chills. By reissuing literary productions from a time period that hasn't received sufficient attention for its contribution to the emergence of science fiction as a recognizable form—one that exists and has meaning in relation to its own traditions and innovations, as well as within a broader ecosystem of literary genres, each of which, as John Rieder notes in *Science Fiction and the Mass Cultural Genre System* (2017), is itself a product of overlapping "communities of practice"—we hope not only to draw attention to key overlooked works but perhaps also to influence the way scholars and sf fans alike think about this crucial yet neglected and misunderstood moment in the emergence of the sf genre.

John W. Campbell and other Cold War–era sf editors and propagandists dubbed a select group of writers and story types from the pulp era to be the golden age of science fiction. In doing so, they helped fix in the popular imagination a too-narrow understanding of what the sf genre can offer. (In his introduction to the 1974 collection *Before the Golden Age*, for example, Isaac Asimov notes that although it may have possessed a certain exuberance, in general sf from before the mid-1930s moment when Campbell assumed editorship of *Astounding Stories* "seems, to anyone who has experienced the Campbell Revolution, to be clumsy, primitive, naive.") By returning to an international tradition of scientific speculation via fiction from after the Poe–Verne–Wells era and before sf's Golden Age, the Radium Age series will demonstrate—contra Asimov et al.—the breadth, richness, and diversity of the literary works that were responding to a vertiginous historical period, and how they helped innovate a nascent genre (which wouldn't be named until the mid-1920s, by Hugo Gernsback, founder of *Amazing Stories* and namesake of the Hugo Awards) as a mode of speculative imagining.

The MIT Press's Noah J. Springer and I are grateful to the sf writers and scholars who have agreed to serve as this series' advisory board. Aided by their guidance, we'll endeavor to surface a rich variety of texts, along with introductions by a diverse group of sf scholars, sf writers, and others that will situate these remarkable, entertaining, forgotten works within their own social, political, and scientific contexts, while drawing out contemporary parallels.

We hope that reading Radium Age writings, published in times as volatile as our own, will serve to remind us that our own era's seemingly natural, eternal, and inevitable social, economic, and cultural forms and norms are—like Madame Curie's atom—forever in flux.

INTRODUCTION

Joshua Glenn

This is the first "Voices of the Radium Age" story collection, which the MIT Press will publish alongside reissued proto-sf novels originally published between 1900 and 1935. As editor of the series and this collection, I hope that readers will come to share my appreciation for what I've dubbed the science fiction genre's formative "Radium Age."

In selecting the stories for our inaugural collection, I wanted to showcase famous authors (e.g., Arthur Conan Doyle, E. M. Forster, Jack London), who, unbeknownst to today's readers, contributed to the emergence of what Hugo Gernsback would name "science fiction." I also wanted to call attention to more obscure writers (e.g., William Hope Hodgson, Neil R. Jones), whose work would prove influential on science fiction's so-called Golden Age. And it was important that the collection also include writers (e.g., Rokeya Sakhawat Hossain, W. E. B. Du Bois) who courageously disrupted the nascent sf genre's mostly white, male, Western fiefdom.

The scholarly aim of this collection, and the series as a whole, is to persuade today's readers that many future-, science-, and technology-oriented "fantastic stories" from circa 1900 to 1935 are not only prescient and provocative but also well written. Our unscholarly aim is simply to entertain: in addition to being of great historical interest, these tales are fun to read!

The author of the earliest story in this collection was a Bengali feminist thinker, writer, educator, and activist. Rokeya Sakhawat Hossain, known after her death as Begum Rokeya (a "begum" is a Muslim woman of high rank), would go on to establish the first school for Muslim girls in Calcutta; and she founded the Muslim Women's Association, which fought for women's education and employment and against extreme forms of purdah. "Sultana's Dream" (published 1905, in the English-language periodical the *Indian Ladies' Magazine*; 1908, in book form) is a feminist utopia that precedes Charlotte Perkins Gilman's *Herland* by a good ten years.

Like the author herself, our narrator, Sultana, is a "purdahnishin"—that is, she practices purdah, whereby women are sequestered in a home's separate "zenana" area. Transported (in a dream, or perhaps she's been summoned into the future by a scientist looking to divert the course of history) to Ladyland, Sultana is at first nervous to venture outside. Isn't it dangerous for women out there? Her female scientist companion, however, reassures her that it's safe . . . because, thirty years earlier, during a war that killed off most of the city-state's menfolk, the surviving men were ordered to isolate themselves indoors. They've remained there ever since.

Fredric Jameson argues persuasively, in *Archaeologies of the Future* (2005), that we should privilege those sf narratives that unveil a vision of a truly different world versus those that merely offer a situation-specific response to a concrete historical dilemma. Regarding the latter, he is thinking of scientific romances like Edward Bellamy's *Looking Backward* and other naive early utopias, as opposed to the wised-up "anti-anti-utopias" of Philip K. Dick, Ursula K. Le Guin, Samuel R. Delany, and other New Wave sf writers of the 1960s and 1970s. Begum Rokeya's story is Bellamy-esque, to be sure, with its weather-controlling technology, solar-powered flying cars, and streets paved with flowers. But it's instructive to revisit the social ills that concerned the author, particularly since we've made so very little progress since then.

The two-hour workday of Ladyland, for example, seems ever less possible for today's workers, who are not only exploited by their employers but bamboozled into believing that "the hustle" is what gives life meaning. And forget about flying cars. When will we ever see realized what Sultana glimpses: the abolition of fossil-fuel technologies, the green-ifying of cities, the detoxification of masculinity, and the triumph of love and truth over fear and hatred?

William Hope Hodgson, whose short story "The Voice in the Night" first appeared in the November 1907 issue of the US pulp magazine *Blue Book*, was an English sailor, bodybuilder, poet, and groundbreaking author of what is now called "weird fiction" and sf. His recurring character Carnacki is a forerunner of occult detectives from Sax Rohmer's Moris Klaw to Douglas Adams's Dirk Gently and Mike Mignola's Hellboy; his novels *The House on the Borderland*

(1908) and *The Night Land* (1912) are required reading; and China Miéville has credited Hodgson with the "weird tentacle" meme later popularized by H. P. Lovecraft.

There are certainly weird tentacles—or pseudopods, perhaps—aplenty in "The Voice in the Night," one of the first-ever yarns about fungal–human symbiosis. A schooner becalmed in an eerie Northern Pacific fog encounters a man, or what's left of one, who rows out to them from a nearby island. He and his fiancée are the survivors of a shipwreck, and the island to which they've drifted on their raft is infected with a lichenous fungus that seems to have sinister intent.

I won't spoil the plot, but suffice it to say the island is a Boschian hellscape where the vile fungus rises "into horrible, fantastic mounds, which seemed almost to quiver, as with a quiet life, when the wind blew across them. . . . Odd places, it appeared as grotesque stunted trees, seeming extraordinarily kinked and gnarled—the whole quaking vilely at times."

Brrr. This story, which was a favorite of Hitchcock's, and which was adapted in 1963 as a Japanese horror movie, is a particularly poignant one during our COVID-19 moment. Realizing that "it would be unallowable to go among healthy humans, with the things from which we were suffering," the stranded couple must decide whether or not to socially isolate . . . forever.

Speaking of social isolation (and fungi), Vashti, protagonist of E. M. Forster's novelette "The Machine Stops" (1909, in *The Oxford and Cambridge Review*; 1928, in the collection *The Eternal Moment and Other Stories*) hasn't exited her room in months. "An armchair is in the centre, by its side a reading-desk—that is all the furniture," we read. "And in the armchair there sits a swaddled lump of flesh—a woman, about five feet high, with a face as white as a fungus."

Is Vashti a prisoner? By no means: She's at liberty to leave her condo underneath Sumatra, and travel the world. Like most of her contemporaries, though, she prefers not to. Twenty years before Aldous Huxley would write *Brave New World*, Forster gives us a dystopian utopia in which one's every physiological, safety, esteem, and self-actualization need is met . . . yet one's social life has been reduced to the equivalent of Snapchat, YouTube, and TED Talks. "She knew several thousand people," we learn of lucky Vashti. The author's wit is at its driest when he goes on to add, "in certain directions human intercourse had advanced enormously."

Living, or at least existing, in a future world, the human population of which has retreated underground, Vashti's prison is an invisible one . . . the bars of which are fashioned by over-solicitous technology, addictive social media, and an idiocracy born of complacency. However, if one attempts to walk upon the surface of the planet, as Vashti's son Kuno insists upon doing, a rhumba of Hodgson-like tentacles—a "Mending Apparatus" prefiguring the writhing mechanical appendages of Terry Gilliam's *Brazil*—will seek you out, ostensibly for your own good.

Responding not only to the administered social order of H. G. Wells's *A Modern Utopia* (1904–1905), but also to his novel *When the Sleeper Wakes* (1899), in which contented Londoners live in a multi-tiered underground society, "The Machine Stops" is one of the most brilliant of the many satires to come—including, in addition to *Brave New World*, Muriel Jaeger's *The Question Mark* (1926), C. S. Lewis's *That Hideous Strength* (1945), and Woody Allen's 1973 sci-fi comedy *Sleeper*—of Wells's technocratic optimism. Written between *A Room With a View* and *Howards End*, when Forster was operating at the peak of his powers, it's an extraordinary achievement.

Uncanny tentacles also play a key role in "The Horror of the Heights" (1913, in *Strand Magazine*), one of a handful of horror and proto-sf stories penned by Arthur Conan Doyle. Doyle's 1910 story "The Terror of Blue John Gap," about a prehistoric creature living beneath an English farm, foreshadows *The Lost World* (1912), in which Professor Challenger and crew seek still-living dinosaurs on an isolated South American plateau. Like *The Lost World* and Doyle's subsequent Professor Challenger stories, not to mention the author's Sherlock Holmes stories, "The Horror of the Heights" is not merely a thriller but an adventure of ratiocination.

Our narrator, whose journal we're reading, is "among the most daring and the most intellectual of flying men." In addition to vying with other fliers to break the height record, Joyce-Armstrong is a seat-of-the-pants scientist—one who, like Challenger, relies on what the semiotician C. S. Peirce named "abductive" reasoning, that is, to hypothesize the unknown cause of a single heterogeneous fact. Curious about why high-flying pilots who'd penetrated the upper atmosphere have died mysteriously (decapitated, covered with slime, gibbering with fright), he posits the existence of stratospheric "air jungles" which telescopes cannot detect.

What makes this a proto-sf story is the logical, rational manner in which our protagonist attempts to make sense of what he happens upon—despite the fact that "greater beauty or greater horror than that," he says, "is not within the ken of man." One is reminded of a line from "The Voice in the Night," regarding the unseen ("invisible") man telling his far-fetched tale: "And with the lightning-like conviction, there came the knowledge that the Invisible was not mad; but sanely facing some intolerable horror." In proposing that although his discoveries are "amazing and even monstrous, it is none the less forcing itself upon the general intelligence that they are true, and that we must readjust our ideas to the new situation," Joyce-Armstrong might well be ventriloquizing Marie Curie, or Albert Einstein, or another pioneering Radium Age scientist.

What, exactly, does he discover? Taking his monoplane up to 40,000 feet, our aeronaut encounters . . . well, I'll just repeat that his experience involves tentacles. Lots of tentacles.

Jack London's posthumously published "The Red One" (1918, in *The Cosmopolitan*, as well as in the collection *The Red One*) is both breathtakingly cosmic in scope, and human—all too disappointingly human. By which I mean to say, the story is not only ethnocentric but also racist.

One could argue that it is our protagonist, the naturalist Bassett, who is at fault, as opposed to the author himself. But the fact remains that the author's description of Balatta, an indigenous Melanesian—"A twisted and wizened complex of apish features, perforated by upturned, sky-open, Mongolian nostrils, by a mouth that sagged from a huge upper-lip and faded precipitately into a retreating chin, by peering querulous eyes that blinked as blink the eyes of denizens of monkey-cages"—is vile. Alas, there's lots more of that sort of thing, here.

In fact, Bassett has arrived in the Solomon Islands aboard a "blackbirder," a ship whose mission it is to coerce islanders to work as slaves or poorly paid laborers in European colonies. Having landed on Guadalcanal, a freak of wind allows him to hear a sound that would normally only be audible deep in the island's interior. A decade before Lovecraft's indescribable "colour out of space," Bassett realizes that there are "no words nor semblances in his vocabulary and experience with which to describe the totality of that sound." Foolishly, he enters the jungle.

I don't think it's giving away too much to say that, after harrowing adventures, a depleted Bassett comes to believe that the sound—which he is informed issues from a sacred, taboo phenomenon known as "the Star-Born"—issues both "deadly whispers of wrath and as equally seductive whispers of delight, striving still to be heard, to convey some cosmic secret, some understanding of infinite import and value." Or that, before he receives his comeuppance at the hands of the natives whom he so despises, he will undergo an experience of the "interfusings and intermating transfusings of matter and force." Far-out stuff, from the author of *White Fang*.

"The Comet," an early example of sf's Afrofuturism subgenre, was the tenth chapter of African American sociologist and civil rights activist W. E. B. Du Bois's *Darkwater: Voices from Within the Veil*. This extraordinary 1920 collection, which interweaves personal essays with fanciful writings, begins with an anti-racist credo: "I believe in God who made of one blood all races that dwell on earth." Du Bois's last-man-on-earth sf story elaborates upon this theme.

When the president of a New York bank—one situated at the intersection of Broadway and Wall Street—needs a man to spelunk the building's Stygian depths in search of old records, he chooses Jim, an African American employee, for this mission. "Of course, they wanted *him* to go down to the lower vaults," Jim reflects with grim fatalism. "It was too dangerous for more valuable men." Ironically, as Jim will soon realize, the vaults are the safest place to be . . . because the tail of a comet that will pass near Earth at noon is composed of poisonous gases.

Returning to the street level, Jim finds out that he's the comet's only survivor—in the entire world, for all he knows. Although devastated by the catastrophe, though, Jim can't help but discern some utopian aspects of his new situation. Like the purdahnishin Sultana, in Rokeya Sakhawat Hossain's story, he finds himself free to move through formerly restricted parts of the city. After washing his face in a drinking fountain (a key signifier of

Jim Crow segregation), he appropriates a meal from an upscale restaurant, plucking it from the hands of a dead waiter: "'Yesterday, they would not have served me,' he whispered, as he forced the food down."

As he roams the eerily silent city, Jim comes across one other survivor, Julia, a wealthy white woman. "Of all the sorts of men she had pictured as coming to her rescue she had not dreamed of one like him. Not that he was not human, but he dwelt in a world so far from hers, so infinitely far, that he seldom even entered her thought." It's the most portentous meet-cute ever . . . but there's no happy ending.

Why not? If this and other Du Bois stories fail to conclude with visions of an anti-racial world, as Hee-Jung Serenity Joo argues in a 2019 *Science Fiction Studies* essay, it's because his utopian politics demand that we readers interrogate our notions of what is possible. However, although Du Bois's proto-*Twilight Zone* parable will conclude in a near-lynching for our hero, at least for one moment—a lyrically described meeting of souls, on a skyscraper rooftop high above New York—a white person will perceive Jim as what he is: a man, first and foremost.

"The Jameson Satellite," which appeared in the July 1931 issue of *Amazing Stories*, is one of scores of pulp sf yarns—including "The Swordsmen of Saturn," "Vampire of the Void," and "The Death's Head Meteor," which, in 1930, was perhaps the first sf story ever to use the term "astronaut"—that Neil R. Jones would crank out during his prolific career. Although known for his (alas, often repetitive) writings from sf's Golden Age, he got his start a few years before then.

Forty million years from now, a crew hailing from the planet Zor, whose inhabitants at some earlier time had "built their own mechanical bodies, and by operation upon one another had removed their brains to the metal heads," come across a satellite orbiting a lifeless Earth. They revive its inhabitant, a cryopreserved Professor Jameson, and transfer his brain into a mechanical body. Although tempted to take the Zoromes up on their offer of "an immortality of never-ending adventures in the vast, endless Universe among the galaxy of stars and planets," as he gazes upon what's left of his planet, Jameson finds himself disconsolate, even suicidal.

"It is all a matter of mental condition," the Zoromes' mission leader, 25X-987, counsels him dispassionately. "Free your mind of this fascinating influence and come with us to visit other worlds, many of them are both beautiful and new. You will then feel a great difference." If I tell you that Jones would go on to write another thirty-odd Professor Jameson stories, then you'll know that the last Earthling takes 25X-987's well-intended, if callous-sounding, advice. Asimov himself would later recount that Jones's Zoromes, who, although technically cyborgs, are robot-like in their emotionless objectivity, were the original source of his "feeling for benevolent robots who could serve man with decency." Benevolent robots—another Radium Age first.

By the way . . . the mechanical body fashioned for Jameson? So many tentacles.

SULTANA'S DREAM

Rokeya Sakhawat Hossain

One evening I was lounging in an easy chair in my bedroom and thinking lazily of the condition of Indian womanhood. I am not sure whether I dozed off or not. But, as far as I remember, I was wide awake. I saw the moonlit sky sparkling with thousands of diamond-like stars, very distinctly.

All of a sudden a lady stood before me; how she came in, I do not know. I took her for my friend, Sister Sara.

"Good morning," said Sister Sara. I smiled inwardly as I knew it was not morning, but starry night. However, I replied to her, saying, "How do you do?"

"I am all right, thank you. Will you please come out and have a look at our garden?"

I looked again at the moon through the open window, and thought there was no harm in going out at that time. The men-servants outside were fast asleep just then, and I could have a pleasant walk with Sister Sara.

I used to have my walks with Sister Sara, when we were at Darjeeling. Many a time did we walk hand in hand and talk light-heartedly in the botanical gardens there. I fancied Sister Sara had probably come to take me to some such garden and I readily accepted her offer and went out with her.

When walking I found to my surprise that it was a fine morning. The town was fully awake and the streets alive with bustling crowds. I was feeling very shy, thinking I was walking in the street in broad daylight, but there was not a single man visible.

Some of the passers-by made jokes at me. Though I could not understand their language, yet I felt sure they were joking. I asked my friend, "What do they say?"

"The women say that you look very mannish."

"Mannish?" said I, "What do they mean by that?"

"They mean that you are shy and timid like men."

"Shy and timid like men?" It was really a joke. I became very nervous, when I found that my companion was not Sister Sara, but a stranger. Oh, what a fool had I been to mistake this lady for my dear old friend, Sister Sara.

She felt my fingers tremble in her hand, as we were walking hand in hand.

"What is the matter, dear?" she said affectionately.

"I feel somewhat awkward," I said in a rather apologizing tone, "as being a purdahnishin woman I am not accustomed to walking about unveiled."

"You need not be afraid of coming across a man here. This is Ladyland, free from sin and harm. Virtue herself reigns here."

By and by I was enjoying the scenery. Really it was very grand. I mistook a patch of green grass for a velvet cushion. Feeling as if I were walking on a soft carpet, I looked down and found the path covered with moss and flowers.

"How nice it is," said I.

"Do you like it?" asked Sister Sara. (I continued calling her "Sister Sara," and she kept calling me by my name.)

"Yes, very much; but I do not like to tread on the tender and sweet flowers."

"Never mind, dear Sultana; your treading will not harm them; they are street flowers."

"The whole place looks like a garden," said I admiringly. "You have arranged every plant so skillfully."

"Your Calcutta could become a nicer garden than this if only your countrymen wanted to make it so."

"They would think it useless to give so much attention to horticulture, while they have so many other things to do."

"They could not find a better excuse," said she with smile.

I became very curious to know where the men were. I met more than a hundred women while walking there, but not a single man.

"Where are the men?" I asked her.

"In their proper places, where they ought to be."

"Pray let me know what you mean by 'their proper places.'"

"O, I see my mistake, you cannot know our customs, as you were never here before. We shut our men indoors."

"Just as we are kept in the zenana?"

"Exactly so."

"How funny," I burst into a laugh. Sister Sara laughed too.

"But dear Sultana, how unfair it is to shut in the harmless women and let loose the men."

"Why? It is not safe for us to come out of the zenana, as we are naturally weak."

"Yes, it is not safe so long as there are men about the streets, nor is it so when a wild animal enters a marketplace."

"Of course not."

"Suppose some lunatics escape from the asylum and begin to do all sorts of mischief to men, horses and other creatures; in that case what will your countrymen do?"

"They will try to capture them and put them back into their asylum."

"Thank you! And you do not think it wise to keep sane people inside an asylum and let loose the insane?"

"Of course not!" said I, laughing lightly.

"As a matter of fact, in your country this very thing is done! Men, who do or at least are capable of doing no end of mischief, are let loose and the innocent women, shut up in the zenana! How can you trust those untrained men out of doors?"

"We have no hand or voice in the management of our social affairs. In India, man is lord and master, he has taken to himself all powers and privileges and shut up the women in the zenana."

"Why do you allow yourselves to be shut up?"

"Because it cannot be helped as they are stronger than women."

"A lion is stronger than a man, but it does not enable him to dominate the human race. You have neglected the duty you owe to yourselves and you have lost your natural rights by shutting your eyes to your own interests."

"But my dear Sister Sara, if we do everything by ourselves, what will the men do then?"

"They should not do anything, excuse me; they are fit for nothing. Only catch them and put them into the zenana."

"But would it be very easy to catch and put them inside the four walls?" said I. "And even if this were done, would all their business—political and commercial—also go with them into the zenana?"

Sister Sara made no reply. She only smiled sweetly. Perhaps she thought it useless to argue with one who was no better than a frog in a well.

By this time we reached Sister Sara's house. It was situated in a beautiful heart-shaped garden. It was a bungalow with a corrugated iron roof. It was cooler and nicer than any of our rich buildings. I cannot begin to describe how neat and how nicely furnished and how tastefully decorated it was.

We sat side by side. She brought out of the parlour a piece of embroidery work and began putting on a fresh design.

"Do you know knitting and needle work?"

"Yes; we have nothing else to do in our zenana."

"But we do not trust our zenana members with embroidery!" she said laughing, "as a man has not patience enough to pass thread through a needlehole even!"

"Have you done all this work yourself?" I asked her, pointing to the various pieces of embroidered teapoy cloths.

"Yes."

"How can you find time to do all these? You have to do the office work as well? Have you not?"

"Yes. I do not stick to the laboratory all day long. I finish my work in two hours."

"In two hours! How do you manage? In our land the officers—magistrates, for instance—work seven hours daily."

"I have seen some of them doing their work. Do you think they work all the seven hours?"

"Certainly they do!"

"No, dear Sultana, they do not. They dawdle away their time in smoking. Some smoke two or three cheroots during the office time. They talk much about their work, but do little. Suppose one cheroot takes half an hour to burn off, and a man smokes twelve cheroots daily; then you see, he wastes six hours every day in sheer smoking."

We talked on various subjects, and I learned that they were not subject to any kind of epidemic disease, nor did they suffer from mosquito bites as we do. I was very much astonished to hear that in Ladyland no one died in youth except by rare accident.

"Will you care to see our kitchen?" she asked me.

"With pleasure," said I, and we went to see it. Of course the men had been asked to clear off when I was going there. The kitchen was situated in a beautiful vegetable garden. Every creeper, every tomato plant was itself an ornament. I found no smoke, nor any chimney either in the kitchen—it was clean and bright; the windows were decorated with flower gardens. There was no sign of coal or fire.

"How do you cook?" I asked.

"With solar heat," she said, at the same time showing me the pipe through which passed the concentrated sunlight and heat. And she cooked something then and there to show me the process.

"How did you manage to gather and store up the sun-heat?" I asked her in amazement.

"Let me tell you a little of our past history then. Thirty years ago, when our present Queen was thirteen years old, she inherited the throne. She was Queen in name only, the Prime Minister really ruling the country.

"Our good Queen liked science very much. She circulated an order that all the women in her country should be educated. Accordingly a number of girls' schools were founded and supported by the government. Education was spread far and wide among women. And early marriage also was stopped. No woman was to be allowed to marry before she was twenty-one. I must tell you that before this change, we had been kept in strict purdah."

"How the tables are turned," I interposed with a laugh.

"But the seclusion is the same," she said. "In a few years we had separate universities, where no men were admitted."

"In the capital, where our Queen lives, there are two universities. One of these invented a wonderful balloon, to which they attached a number of pipes. By means of this captive balloon which they managed to keep afloat above the cloud-land, they could draw as much water from the atmosphere as they pleased. As the water was incessantly being drawn by the university people, no cloud gathered and the ingenious Lady Principal stopped rain and storms thereby."

"Really! Now I understand why there is no mud here!" said I. But I could not understand how it was possible to accumulate water in the pipes. She explained to me how it was done, but I was unable to understand her, as my scientific knowledge was very limited. However, she went on, "When the other university came to know of this, they became exceedingly jealous and tried to do something more extraordinary still. They invented an instrument by which they could collect as much sun-heat as they wanted. And they kept the heat stored up to be distributed among others as required.

"While the women were engaged in scientific research, the men of this country were busy increasing their military power. When they came to know that the female universities were able to draw water from the atmosphere and collect heat from the sun, they only laughed at the members of the universities and called the whole thing 'a sentimental nightmare'!"

"Your achievements are very wonderful indeed! But tell me how you managed to put the men of your country into the zenana. Did you entrap them first?"

"No."

"It is not likely that they would surrender their free and open air life of their own accord and confine themselves within the four walls of the zenana! They must have been overpowered."

"Yes, they have been!"

"By whom? By some lady-warriors, I suppose?"

"No, not by arms."

"Yes, it cannot be so. Men's arms are stronger than women's. Then?"

"By brain."

"Even their brains are bigger and heavier than women's. Are they not?"

“Yes, but what of that? An elephant also has got a bigger and heavier brain than a man has. Yet man can enchain elephants and employ them, according to their own wishes.”

“Well said, but tell me please, how it all actually happened. I am dying to know it!”

“Women’s brains are somewhat quicker than men’s. Ten years ago, when the military officers called our scientific discoveries ‘a sentimental nightmare,’ some of the young ladies wanted to say something in reply to those remarks. But both the Lady Principals restrained them and said they should reply not by word, but by deed, if ever they got the opportunity. And they had not long to wait for that opportunity.”

“How marvelous!” I heartily clapped my hands. “And now the proud gentlemen are dreaming sentimental dreams themselves.”

“Soon afterwards, certain persons came from a neighbouring country and took shelter in ours. They were in trouble, having committed some political offense. The king who cared more for power than for good government asked our kind-hearted Queen to hand them over to his officers. She refused, as it was against her principle to turn out refugees. For this refusal the king declared war against our country.

“Our military officers sprang to their feet at once and marched out to meet the enemy. The enemy however, was too strong for them. Our soldiers fought bravely, no doubt. But in spite of all their bravery the foreign army advanced step by step to invade our country.

"Nearly all the men had gone out to fight; even a boy of sixteen was not left home. Most of our warriors were killed, the rest driven back and the enemy came within twenty-five miles of the capital.

"A meeting of a number of wise ladies was held at the Queen's palace to advise as to what should be done to save the land. Some proposed to fight like soldiers; others objected and said that women were not trained to fight with swords and guns, nor were they accustomed to fighting with any weapons. A third party regretfully remarked that they were hopelessly weak of body.

"'If you cannot save your country for lack of physical strength,' said the Queen, 'try to do so by brain power.'"

"There was a dead silence for a few minutes. Her Royal Highness said again, 'I must commit suicide if the land and my honour are lost.'"

"Then the Lady Principal of the second university (who had collected sun-heat), who had been silently thinking during the consultation, remarked that they were all but lost, and there was little hope left for them. There was, however, one plan which she would like to try, and this would be her first and last efforts; if she failed in this, there would be nothing left but to commit suicide. All present solemnly vowed that they would never allow themselves to be enslaved, no matter what happened.

"The Queen thanked them heartily, and asked the Lady Principal to try her plan. The Lady Principal rose again and said, 'Before we go out, the men must enter the zenanas. I make this prayer for the sake of purdah.' 'Yes, of course,' replied Her Royal Highness.

"On the following day the Queen called upon all men to retire into zenanas for the sake of honour and liberty. Wounded and tired as they were, they took that order rather for a boon! They bowed low and entered the zenanas without uttering a single word of protest. They were sure that there was no hope for this country at all.

"Then the Lady Principal with her two thousand students marched to the battle field, and, arriving there, directed all the rays of the concentrated sunlight and heat towards the enemy.

"The heat and light were too much for them to bear. They all ran away panic-stricken, not knowing in their bewilderment how to counteract that scorching heat. When they fled away, leaving their guns and other ammunitions of war, they were burnt down by means of the same sun-heat. Since then no one has tried to invade our country any more."

"And since then your countrymen never tried to come out of the zenana?"

"Yes, they wanted to be free. Some of the police commissioners and district magistrates sent word to the Queen to the effect that the military officers certainly deserved to be imprisoned for their failure; but they had never neglected their duty and therefore they should not be punished, and they prayed to be restored to their respective offices.

"Her Royal Highness sent them a circular letter intimating to them that if their services should ever be needed they would be sent for, and that in the meanwhile they should remain where they were. Now that they are accustomed to the purdah system and have ceased to grumble at their seclusion, we call the system 'Mardana' instead of 'zenana.'"

"But how do you manage," I asked Sister Sara, "to do without the police or magistrates in case of theft or murder?"

"Since the 'Mardana' system has been established, there has been no more crime or sin; therefore we do not require a policeman to find out a culprit, nor do we want a magistrate to try a criminal case."

"That is very good, indeed. I suppose if there was any dishonest person, you could very easily chastise her. As you gained a decisive victory without shedding a single drop of blood, you could drive off crime and criminals too without much difficulty!"

"Now, dear Sultana, will you sit here or come to my parlour?" she asked me.

"Your kitchen is not inferior to a queen's boudoir!" I replied with a pleasant smile, "but we must leave it now; for the gentlemen may be cursing me for keeping them away from their duties in the kitchen so long." We both laughed heartily.

"How my friends at home will be amused and amazed, when I go back and tell them that in the far-off Ladyland, ladies rule over the country and control all social matters, while gentlemen are kept in the Mardanas to mind babies, to cook and to do all sorts of domestic work; and that cooking is so easy a thing that it is simply a pleasure to cook!"

"Yes, tell them about all that you see here."

"Please let me know, how you carry on land cultivation and how you plough the land and do other hard manual work."

"Our fields are tilled by means of electricity, which supplies motive power for other hard work as well, and we employ it for our aerial conveyances too. We have no rail road nor any paved streets here."

"Therefore neither street nor railway accidents occur here," said I. "Do not you ever suffer from want of rainwater?" I asked.

"Never since the 'water balloon' has been set up. You see the big balloon and pipes attached thereto. By their aid we can draw as much rainwater as we require. Nor do we ever suffer from flood or thunderstorms. We are all very busy making nature yield as much as she can. We do not find time to quarrel with one another, as we never sit idle. Our noble Queen is exceedingly fond of botany; it is her ambition to convert the whole country into one grand garden."

"The idea is excellent. What is your chief food?"

"Fruits."

"How do you keep your country cool in hot weather? We regard the rainfall in summer as a blessing from heaven."

"When the heat becomes unbearable, we sprinkle the ground with plentiful showers drawn from the artificial fountains. And in cold weather we keep our room warm with sun-heat."

She showed me her bathroom, the roof of which was removable. She could enjoy a shower bath whenever she liked, by simply removing the roof (which was like the lid of a box) and turning on the tap of the shower pipe.

"You are a lucky people!" ejaculated I. "You know no want. What is your religion, may I ask?"

"Our religion is based on Love and Truth. It is our religious duty to love one another and to be absolutely truthful. If any person lies, she or he is . . ."

"Punished with death?"

"No, not with death. We do not take pleasure in killing a creature of God, especially a human being. The liar is asked to leave this land for good and never to come to it again."

"Is an offender never forgiven?"

"Yes, if that person repents sincerely."

"Are you not allowed to see any man, except your own relations?"

"No one except sacred relations."

"Our circle of sacred relations is very limited; even first cousins are not sacred."

"But ours is very large; a distant cousin is as sacred as a brother."

"That is very good. I see purity itself reigns over your land. I should like to see the good Queen, who is so sagacious and far-sighted and who has made all these rules."

"All right," said Sister Sara.

Then she screwed a couple of seats onto a square piece of plank. To this plank she attached two smooth and well-polished balls. When I asked her what the balls were for, she said they were hydrogen balls and they were used to overcome the force of gravity. The balls were of different capacities to be used according to the different weights desired to be overcome. She then fastened to the air-car two wing-like blades, which, she said, were worked by electricity. After we were comfortably seated she touched a knob and the blades began to whirl, moving faster and faster every moment. At first we were raised to the height of about six or seven feet and then off we flew. And before I could realize that we had commenced moving, we reached the garden of the Queen.

My friend lowered the air-car by reversing the action of the machine, and when the car touched the ground, the machine was stopped and we got out.

I had seen from the air-car the Queen walking on a garden path with her little daughter (who was four years old) and her maids of honour.

"Halloo! You here!" cried the Queen, addressing Sister Sara. I was introduced to Her Royal Highness and was received by her cordially without any ceremony.

I was very much delighted to make her acquaintance. In the course of the conversation I had with her, the Queen told me that she had no objection to permitting her subjects to trade with other countries. "But," she continued, "no trade was possible with countries where the women were kept in the zenanas and so unable to come and trade with us. Men, we find, are rather of lower morals and so we do not like dealing with them. We do not covet other people's land, we do not fight for a piece of diamond though it may be a thousand-fold brighter than the Koh-i-Noor, nor do we grudge a ruler his Peacock Throne. We dive deep into the ocean of knowledge and try to find out the precious gems, which nature has kept in store for us. We enjoy nature's gifts as much as we can."

After taking leave of the Queen, I visited the famous universities, and was shown some of their manufactories, laboratories and observatories.

After visiting the above places of interest we got again into the air-car, but as soon as it began moving, I somehow slipped down and the fall startled me out of my dream. And on opening my eyes, I found myself in my own bedroom still lounging in the easy chair!

1905

THE VOICE IN THE NIGHT

William Hope Hodgson

It was a dark, starless night. We were becalmed in the Northern Pacific. Our exact position I do not know; for the sun had been hidden during the course of a weary, breathless week, by a thin haze which had seemed to float above us, about the height of our mastheads, at whiles descending and shrouding the surrounding sea.

With there being no wind, we had steadied the tiller, and I was the only man on deck. The crew, consisting of two men and a boy, were sleeping forrard in their den; while Will—my friend, and the master of our little craft—was aft in his bunk on the port side of the little cabin.

Suddenly, from out of the surrounding darkness, there came a hail: "Schooner, ahoy!"

The cry was so unexpected that I gave no immediate answer, because of my surprise.

It came again—a voice curiously throaty and inhuman, calling from somewhere upon the dark sea away on our port broadside: "Schooner, ahoy!"

"Hullo!" I sung out, having gathered my wits somewhat. "What are you? What do you want?"

"You need not be afraid," answered the queer voice, having probably noticed some trace of confusion in my tone. "I am only an old man."

The pause sounded oddly; but it was only afterwards that it came back to me with any significance.

"Why don't you come alongside, then?" I queried somewhat snappishly; for I liked not his hinting at my having been a trifle shaken.

"I—I—can't. It wouldn't be safe. I——" The voice broke off, and there was silence.

"What do you mean?" I asked, growing more and more astonished. "Why not safe? Where are you?"

I listened for a moment; but there came no answer. And then, a sudden indefinite suspicion, of I knew not what, coming to me, I stepped swiftly to the binnacle, and took out the lighted lamp. At the same time, I knocked on the deck with my heel to waken Will. Then I was back at the side, throwing the yellow funnel of light out into the silent immensity beyond our rail. As I did so, I heard a slight, muffled cry, and then the sound of a splash as though someone had dipped oars abruptly. Yet I cannot say that I saw anything with certainty; save, it seemed to me, that with the first flash of the light, there had been something upon the waters, where now there was nothing.

"Hullo, there!" I called. "What foolery is this!"

But there came only the indistinct sounds of a boat being pulled away into the night.

Then I heard Will's voice, from the direction of the after scuttle: "What's up, George?"

"Come here, Will!" I said.

"What is it?" he asked, coming across the deck.

I told him the queer thing which had happened. He put several questions; then, after a moment's silence, he raised his hands to his lips, and hailed: "Boat, ahoy!"

From a long distance away there came back to us a faint reply, and my companion repeated his call. Presently, after a short period of silence, there grew on our hearing the muffled sound of oars; at which Will hailed again.

This time there was a reply: "Put away the light."

"I'm damned if I will," I muttered; but Will told me to do as the voice bade, and I shoved it down under the bulwarks.

"Come nearer," he said, and the oar-strokes continued. Then, when apparently some half-dozen fathoms distant, they again ceased.

"Come alongside," exclaimed Will. "There's nothing to be frightened of aboard here!"

"Promise that you will not show the light?"

"What's to do with you," I burst out, "that you're so infernally afraid of the light?"

"Because——" began the voice, and stopped short.

"Because what?" I asked quickly.

Will put his hand on my shoulder.

"Shut up a minute, old man," he said, in a low voice. "Let me tackle him."

He leant more over the rail.

"See here, Mister," he said, "this is a pretty queer business, you coming upon us like this, right out in the middle of the blessed Pacific. How are we to know what sort of a hanky-panky trick you're up to? You say there's only one of you. How are we to know, unless we get a squint at you—eh? What's your objection to the light, anyway?"

As he finished, I heard the noise of the oars again, and then the voice came; but now from a greater distance, and sounding extremely hopeless and pathetic.

"I am sorry—sorry! I would not have troubled you, only I am hungry, and—so is she."

The voice died away, and the sound of the oars, dipping irregularly, was borne to us.

"Stop!" sung out Will. "I don't want to drive you away. Come back! We'll keep the light hidden, if you don't like it."

He turned to me: "It's a damned queer rig, this; but I think there's nothing to be afraid of?"

There was a question in his tone, and I replied.

"No, I think the poor devil's been wrecked around here, and gone crazy."

The sound of the oars drew nearer.

"Shove that lamp back in the binnacle," said Will; then he leaned over the rail and listened. I replaced the lamp, and came back to his side. The dipping of the oars ceased some dozen yards distant.

"Won't you come alongside now?" asked Will in an even voice. "I have had the lamp put back in the binnacle."

"I—I cannot," replied the voice. "I dare not come nearer. I dare not even pay you for the—the provisions."

"That's all right," said Will, and hesitated. "You're welcome to as much grub as you can take——" Again he hesitated.

"You are very good," exclaimed the voice. "May God, Who understands everything, reward you——" It broke off huskily.

“The—the lady?” said Will abruptly. “Is she——”

“I have left her behind upon the island,” came the voice.

“What island?” I cut in. “I know not its name,” returned the voice. “I would to God——!” it began, and checked itself as suddenly.

“Could we not send a boat for her?” asked Will at this point.

“No!” said the voice, with extraordinary emphasis. “My God! No!” There was a moment’s pause; then it added, in a tone which seemed a merited reproach: “It was because of our want I ventured—because her agony tortured me.”

“I am a forgetful brute,” exclaimed Will. “Just wait a minute, whoever you are, and I will bring you up something at once.”

In a couple of minutes he was back again, and his arms were full of various edibles. He paused at the rail.

“Can’t you come alongside for them?” he asked.

“No—I dare not,” replied the voice, and it seemed to me that in its tones I detected a note of stifled craving—as though the owner hushed a mortal desire. It came to me then in a flash, that the poor old creature out there in the darkness, was suffering for actual need of that which Will held in his arms; and yet, because of some unintelligible dread, refraining from dashing to the side of our little schooner, and receiving it. And with the lightning-like conviction, there came the knowledge that the Invisible was not mad; but sanely facing some intolerable horror.

“Damn it, Will!” I said, full of many feelings, over which predominated a vast sympathy. “Get a box. We must float off the stuff to him in it.”

This we did—propelling it away from the vessel, out into the darkness, by means of a boathook. In a minute, a slight cry from the Invisible came to us, and we knew that he had secured the box.

A little later, he called out a farewell to us, and so heartful a blessing, that I am sure we were the better for it. Then, without more ado, we heard the ply of oars across the darkness.

"Pretty soon off," remarked Will, with perhaps just a little sense of injury.

"Wait," I replied. "I think somehow he'll come back. He must have been badly needing that food."

"And the lady," said Will. For a moment he was silent; then he continued: "It's the queerest thing ever I've tumbled across, since I've been fishing."

"Yes," I said, and fell to pondering.

And so the time slipped away—an hour, another, and still Will stayed with me; for the queer adventure had knocked all desire for sleep out of him.

The third hour was three parts through, when we heard again the sound of oars across the silent ocean.

"Listen!" said Will, a low note of excitement in his voice.

"He's coming, just as I thought," I muttered.

The dipping of the oars grew nearer, and I noted that the strokes were firmer and longer. The food had been needed.

They came to a stop a little distance off the broadside, and the queer voice came again to us through the darkness: "Schooner, ahoy!"

"That you?" asked Will.

"Yes," replied the voice. "I left you suddenly; but—but there was great need."

"The lady?" questioned Will.

"The—lady is grateful now on earth. She will be more grateful soon in—in heaven."

Will began to make some reply, in a puzzled voice; but became confused, and broke off short. I said nothing. I was wondering at the curious pauses, and, apart from my wonder, I was full of a great sympathy.

The voice continued: "We—she and I, have talked, as we shared the result of God's tenderness and yours——"

Will interposed; but without coherence.

"I beg of you not to—to belittle your deed of Christian charity this night," said the voice. "Be sure that it has not escaped His notice."

It stopped, and there was a full minute's silence. Then it came again: "We have spoken together upon that which—which has befallen us. We had thought to go out, without telling any, of the terror which has come into our—lives. She is with me in believing that to-night's happenings are under a special ruling, and that it is God's wish that we should tell to you all that we have suffered since—since——"

"Yes?" said Will softly.

"Since the sinking of the *Albatross*."

"Ah!" I exclaimed involuntarily. "She left Newcastle for 'Frisco some six months ago, and hasn't been heard of since."

"Yes," answered the voice. "But some few degrees to the North of the line she was caught in a terrible storm, and dismasted. When the day came, it was found that she was leaking badly, and, presently, it falling to a calm, the sailors took to the boats, leaving—leaving a young lady—my fiancée—and myself upon the wreck.

"We were below, gathering together a few of our belongings, when they left. They were entirely callous, through fear, and when we came up upon the deck, we saw them only as small shapes afar off upon the horizon. Yet we did not despair, but set to work and constructed a small raft. Upon this we put such few matters as it would hold including a quantity of water and some ship's biscuit. Then, the vessel being very deep in the water, we got ourselves on to the raft, and pushed off.

"It was later, when I observed that we seemed to be in the way of some tide or current, which bore us from the ship at an angle; so that in the course of three hours, by my watch, her hull became invisible to our sight, her broken masts remaining in view for a somewhat longer period. Then, towards evening, it grew misty, and so through the night. The next day we were still encompassed by the mist, the weather remaining quiet.

"For four days we drifted through this strange haze, until, on the evening of the fourth day, there grew upon our ears the murmur of breakers at a distance. Gradually it became plainer, and, somewhat after midnight, it appeared to sound upon either hand at no very great space. The raft was raised upon a swell several times, and then we were in smooth water, and the noise of the breakers was behind.

"When the morning came, we found that we were in a sort of great lagoon; but of this we noticed little at the time; for close before us, through the enshrouding mist, loomed the hull of a large sailing-vessel. With one accord, we fell upon our knees and thanked God; for we thought that here was an end to our perils. We had much to learn.

"The raft drew near to the ship, and we shouted on them to take us aboard; but none answered. Presently the raft touched against the side of the vessel, and, seeing a rope hanging downwards, I seized it and began to climb. Yet I had much ado to make my way up, because of a kind of grey, lichenous fungus which had seized upon the rope, and which blotched the side of the ship lividly.

"I reached the rail and clambered over it, on to the deck. Here I saw that the decks were covered, in great patches, with grey masses, some of them rising into nodules several feet in height; but at the time I thought less of this matter than of the possibility of there being people aboard the ship. I shouted; but none answered. Then I went to the door below the poop deck. I opened it, and peered in. There was a great smell of staleness, so that I knew in a moment that nothing living was within, and with the knowledge, I shut the door quickly; for I felt suddenly lonely.

"I went back to the side where I had scrambled up. My—my sweetheart was still sitting quietly upon the raft. Seeing me look down she called up to know whether there were any aboard of the ship. I replied that the vessel had the appearance of having been long deserted; but that if she would wait a little I would see whether there was anything in the shape of a ladder by which she could ascend to the deck. Then we would make a search through the vessel together. A little later, on the opposite side of the decks, I found a rope side-ladder. This I carried across, and a minute afterwards she was beside me.

"Together we explored the cabins and apartments in the after part of the ship; but nowhere was there any sign of life. Here and there within the cabins themselves, we came across odd patches of that queer fungus; but this, as my sweetheart said, could be cleansed away.

"In the end, having assured ourselves that the after portion of the vessel was empty, we picked our ways to the bows, between the ugly grey nodules of that strange growth; and here we made a further search which told us that there was indeed none aboard but ourselves.

"This being now beyond any doubt, we returned to the stern of the ship and proceeded to make ourselves as comfortable as possible. Together we cleared out and cleaned two of the cabins: and after that I made examination whether there was anything eatable in the ship. This I soon found was so, and thanked God in my heart for His goodness. In addition to this I discovered the whereabouts of the fresh-water pump, and having fixed it I found the water drinkable, though somewhat unpleasant to the taste.

"For several days we stayed aboard the ship, without attempting to get to the shore. We were busily engaged in making the place habitable. Yet even thus early we became aware that our lot was even less to be desired than might have been imagined; for though, as a first step, we scraped away the odd patches of growth that studded the floors and walls of the cabins and saloon, yet they returned almost to their original size within the space of twenty-four hours, which not only discouraged us, but gave us a feeling of vague unease.

"Still we would not admit ourselves beaten, so set to work afresh, and not only scraped away the fungus, but soaked the places where it had been, with carbolic, a can-full of which I had found in the pantry. Yet, by the end of the week the growth had returned in full strength, and, in addition, it had spread to other places, as though our touching it had allowed germs from it to travel elsewhere.

"On the seventh morning, my sweetheart woke to find a small patch of it growing on her pillow, close to her face. At that, she came to me, so soon as she could get her garments upon her. I was in the galley, at the time, lighting the fire for breakfast.

"'Come here, John,' she said, and led me aft. When I saw the thing upon her pillow I shuddered, and then and there we agreed to go right out of the ship and see whether we could not fare to make ourselves more comfortable ashore.

"Hurriedly we gathered together our few belongings, and even among these I found that the fungus had been at work; for one of her shawls had a little lump of it growing near one edge. I threw the whole thing over the side, without saying anything to her.

"The raft was still alongside, but it was too clumsy to guide, and I lowered down a small boat that hung across the stern, and in this we made our way to the shore. Yet, as we drew near to it, I became gradually aware that here the vile fungus, which had driven us from the ship, was growing riot. In places it rose into horrible, fantastic mounds, which seemed almost to quiver, as with a quiet life, when the wind blew across them. Here and there it took on the forms of vast fingers, and in others it just spread out flat and smooth and treacherous. Odd places, it appeared as grotesque stunted trees, seeming extraordinarily kinked and gnarled—the whole quaking vilely at times.

"At first, it seemed to us that there was no single portion of the surrounding shore which was not hidden beneath the masses of the hideous lichen; yet, in this, I found we were mistaken; for somewhat later, coasting along the shore at a little distance, we descried a smooth white patch of what appeared to be fine sand, and there we landed. It was not sand. What it was I do not know. All that I have observed is that upon it the fungus will not grow; while everywhere else, save where the sand-like earth wanders oddly, path-wise, amid the grey desolation of the lichen, there is nothing but that loathsome greyness.

"It is difficult to make you understand how cheered we were to find one place that was absolutely free from the growth, and here we deposited our belongings. Then we went back to the ship for such things as it seemed to us we should need. Among other matters, I managed to bring ashore with me one of the ship's sails, with which I constructed two small tents, which, though exceedingly rough-shaped, served the purpose for which they were intended. In these we lived and stored our various necessities, and thus for a matter of some four weeks all went smoothly and without particular unhappiness. Indeed,

I may say with much of happiness—for—for we were together.

"It was on the thumb of her right hand that the growth first showed. It was only a small circular spot, much like a little grey mole. My God! how the fear leapt to my heart when she showed me the place. We cleansed it, between us, washing it with carbolic and water. In the morning of the following day she showed her hand to me again. The grey warty thing had returned. For a little while, we looked at one another in silence. Then, still wordless, we started again to remove it. In the midst of the operation she spoke suddenly.

"'What's that on the side of your face, dear?' Her voice was sharp with anxiety. I put my hand up to feel.

"'There! Under the hair by your ear. A little to the front a bit.' My finger rested upon the place, and then I knew.

"'Let us get your thumb done first,' I said. And she submitted, only because she was afraid to touch me until it was cleansed. I finished washing and disinfecting her thumb, and then she turned to my face. After it was finished we sat together and talked awhile of many things for there had come into our lives sudden, very terrible thoughts. We were, all at once, afraid of something worse than death. We spoke of loading the boat with provisions and water and making our way out on to the sea; yet we were helpless, for many causes, and—and the growth had attacked us already. We decided to stay. God would do with us what was His will. We would wait.

"A month, two months, three months passed and the places grew somewhat, and there had come others. Yet we fought so strenuously with the fear that its headway was but slow, comparatively speaking.

"Occasionally we ventured off to the ship for such stores as we needed. There we found that the fungus grew persistently. One of the nodules on the maindeck became soon as high as my head.

"We had now given up all thought or hope of leaving the island. We had realized that it would be unallowable to go among healthy humans, with the things from which we were suffering.

"With this determination and knowledge in our minds we knew that we should have to husband our food and water; for we did not know, at that time, but that we should possibly live for many years.

"This reminds me that I have told you that I am an old man. Judged by the years this is not so. But—but——"

He broke off; then continued somewhat abruptly: "As I was saying, we knew that we should have to use care in the matter of food. But we had no idea then how little food there was left of which to take care. It was a week later that I made the discovery that all the other bread tanks—which I had supposed full—were empty, and that (beyond odd tins of vegetables and meat, and some other matters) we had nothing on which to depend, but the bread in the tank which I had already opened.

"After learning this I bestirred myself to do what I could, and set to work at fishing in the lagoon; but with no success. At this I was somewhat inclined to feel desperate until the thought came to me to try outside the lagoon, in the open sea.

"Here, at times, I caught odd fish; but so infrequently that they proved of but little help in keeping us from the hunger which threatened.

"It seemed to me that our deaths were likely to come by hunger, and not by the growth of the thing which had seized upon our bodies.

"We were in this state of mind when the fourth month wore out. When I made a very horrible discovery. One morning, a little before midday, I came off from the ship with a portion of the biscuits which were left. In the mouth of her tent I saw my sweetheart sitting, eating something.

"'What is it, my dear?' I called out as I leapt ashore. Yet, on hearing my voice, she seemed confused, and, turning, slyly threw something towards the edge of the little clearing. It fell short, and a vague suspicion having arisen within me, I walked across and picked it up. It was a piece of the grey fungus.

"As I went to her with it in my hand, she turned deadly pale; then rose red.

"I felt strangely dazed and frightened.

"'My dear! My dear!' I said, and could say no more. Yet at these words she broke down and cried bitterly. Gradually, as she calmed, I got from her the news that she had tried it the preceding day, and—and liked it. I got her to promise on her knees not to touch it again, however great our hunger. After she had promised she told me that the desire for it had come suddenly, and that, until the moment of desire, she had experienced nothing towards it but the most extreme repulsion.

"Later in the day, feeling strangely restless, and much shaken with the thing which I had discovered, I made my way along one of the twisted paths—formed by the white, sand-like substance—which led among the fungoid growth. I had, once before, ventured along there; but not to any great distance. This time, being involved in perplexing thought, I went much further than hitherto.

"Suddenly I was called to myself by a queer hoarse sound on my left. Turning quickly I saw that there was movement among an extraordinarily shaped mass of fungus, close to my elbow. It was swaying uneasily, as though it possessed life of its own. Abruptly, as I stared, the thought came to me that the thing had a grotesque resemblance to the figure of a distorted human creature. Even as the fancy flashed into my brain, there was a slight, sickening noise of tearing, and I saw that one of the branch-like arms was detaching itself from the surrounding grey masses, and coming towards me. The head of the thing—a shapeless grey ball, inclined in my direction. I stood stupidly, and the vile arm brushed across my face. I gave out a frightened cry, and ran back a few paces. There was a sweetish taste upon my lips where the thing had touched me. I licked them, and was immediately filled with an inhuman desire. I turned and seized a mass of the fungus. Then more and—more. I was insatiable. In the midst of devouring, the remembrance of the morning's discovery swept into my mazed brain. It was sent by God. I dashed the fragment I held to the ground. Then, utterly wretched and feeling a dreadful guiltiness, I made my way back to the little encampment.

"I think she knew, by some marvellous intuition which love must have given, so soon as she set eyes on me. Her quiet sympathy made it easier for me, and I told her of my sudden weakness; yet omitted to mention the extraordinary thing which had gone before. I desired to spare her all unnecessary terror.

"But, for myself, I had added an intolerable knowledge, to breed an incessant terror in my brain; for I doubted not but that I had seen the end of one of those men who had come to the island in the ship in the lagoon; and in that monstrous ending I had seen our own.

"Thereafter we kept from the abominable food, though the desire for it had entered into our blood. Yet our drear punishment was upon us; for, day by day, with monstrous rapidity, the fungoid growth took hold of our poor bodies. Nothing we could do would check it materially, and so—and so—we who had been human, became—Well, it matters less each day. Only—only we had been man and maid!

"And day by day the fight is more dreadful, to withstand the hungerlust for the terrible lichen.

"A week ago we ate the last of the biscuit, and since that time I have caught three fish. I was out here fishing tonight when your schooner drifted upon me out of the mist. I hailed you. You know the rest, and may God, out of His great heart, bless you for your goodness to a—a couple of poor outcast souls."

There was the dip of an oar—another. Then the voice came again, and for the last time, sounding through the slight surrounding mist, ghostly and mournful.

"God bless you! Good-bye!"

"Good-bye," we shouted together, hoarsely, our hearts full of many emotions.

I glanced about me. I became aware that the dawn was upon us.

The sun flung a stray beam across the hidden sea; pierced the mist dully, and lit up the receding boat with a gloomy fire. Indistinctly I saw something nodding between the oars. I thought of a sponge—a great, grey nodding sponge. The oars continued to ply. They were grey—as was the boat—and my eyes searched a moment vainly for the conjunction of hand and oar. My gaze flashed back to the—head. It nodded forward as the oars went backward for the stroke. Then the oars were dipped, the boat shot out of the patch of light, and the—the thing went nodding into the mist.

1907

THE MACHINE STOPS

E. M. Forster

Part I: The Air-Ship

Imagine, if you can, a small room, hexagonal in shape, like the cell of a bee. It is lighted neither by window nor by lamp, yet it is filled with a soft radiance. There are no apertures for ventilation, yet the air is fresh. There are no musical instruments, and yet, at the moment that my meditation opens, this room is throbbing with melodious sounds. An armchair is in the centre, by its side a reading-desk—that is all the furniture. And in the armchair there sits a swaddled lump of flesh—a woman, about five feet high, with a face as white as a fungus. It is to her that the little room belongs.

An electric bell rang.

The woman touched a switch and the music was silent.

"I suppose I must see who it is," she thought, and set her chair in motion. The chair, like the music, was worked by machinery and it rolled her to the other side of the room where the bell still rang importunately.

"Who is it?" she called. Her voice was irritable, for she had been interrupted often since the music began. She knew several thousand people; in certain directions human intercourse had advanced enormously.

But when she listened into the receiver, her white face wrinkled into smiles, and she said:

"Very well. Let us talk, I will isolate myself. I do not expect anything important will happen for the next five minutes—for I can give you fully five minutes, Kuno. Then I must deliver my lecture on 'Music during the Australian Period.'"

She touched the isolation knob, so that no one else could speak to her. Then she touched the lighting apparatus, and the little room was plunged into darkness.

"Be quick!" She called, her irritation returning. "Be quick, Kuno; here I am in the dark wasting my time."

But it was fully fifteen seconds before the round plate that she held in her hands began to glow. A faint blue light shot across it, darkening to purple, and presently she could see the image of her son, who lived on the other side of the earth, and he could see her.

"Kuno, how slow you are."

He smiled gravely.

"I really believe you enjoy dawdling."

"I have called you before, mother, but you were always busy or isolated. I have something particular to say."

"What is it, dearest boy? Be quick. Why could you not send it by pneumatic post?"

"Because I prefer saying such a thing. I want—"

"Well?"

"I want you to come and see me."

Vashti watched his face in the blue plate.

"But I can see you!" she exclaimed. "What more do you want?"

"I want to see you not through the Machine," said Kuno. "I want to speak to you not through the wearisome Machine."

"Oh, hush!" said his mother, vaguely shocked. "You mustn't say anything against the Machine."

"Why not?"

"One mustn't."

"You talk as if a god had made the Machine," cried the other. "I believe that you pray to it when you are unhappy. Men made it, do not forget that. Great men, but men. The Machine is much, but it is not everything. I see something like you in this plate, but I do not see you. I hear something like you through this telephone, but I do not hear you. That is why I want you to come. Pay me a visit, so that we can meet face to face, and talk about the hopes that are in my mind."

She replied that she could scarcely spare the time for a visit.

"The air-ship barely takes two days to fly between me and you."

"I dislike air-ships."

"Why?"

"I dislike seeing the horrible brown earth, and the sea, and the stars when it is dark. I get no ideas in an air-ship."

"I do not get them anywhere else."

"What kind of ideas can the air give you?"

He paused for an instant.

"Do you not know four big stars that form an oblong, and three stars close together in the middle of the oblong, and hanging from these stars, three other stars?"

"No, I do not. I dislike the stars. But did they give you an idea? How interesting; tell me."

"I had an idea that they were like a man."

"I do not understand."

"The four big stars are the man's shoulders and his knees. The three stars in the middle are like the belts that men wore once, and the three stars hanging are like a sword."

"A sword?"

"Men carried swords about with them, to kill animals and other men."

"It does not strike me as a very good idea, but it is certainly original. When did it come to you first?"

"In the air-ship—" He broke off, and she fancied that he looked sad. She could not be sure, for the Machine did not transmit nuances of expression. It only gave a general idea of people—an idea that was good enough for all practical purposes, Vashti thought. The imponderable bloom, declared by a discredited philosophy to be the actual essence of intercourse, was rightly ignored by the Machine, just as the imponderable bloom of the grape was ignored by the manufacturers of artificial fruit. Something "good enough" had long since been accepted by our race.

"The truth is," he continued, "that I want to see these stars again. They are curious stars. I want to see them not from the air-ship, but from the surface of the earth, as our ancestors did, thousands of years ago. I want to visit the surface of the earth."

She was shocked again.

"Mother, you must come, if only to explain to me what is the harm of visiting the surface of the earth."

"No harm," she replied, controlling herself. "But no advantage. The surface of the earth is only dust and mud, no advantage. The surface of the earth is only dust and mud, no life remains on it, and you would need a respirator, or the cold of the outer air would kill you. One dies immediately in the outer air."

"I know; of course I shall take all precautions."

"And besides—"

"Well?"

She considered, and chose her words with care. Her son had a queer temper, and she wished to dissuade him from the expedition.

"It is contrary to the spirit of the age," she asserted.

"Do you mean by that, contrary to the Machine?"

"In a sense, but—"

His image in the blue plate faded.

"Kuno!"

He had isolated himself.

For a moment Vashti felt lonely.

Then she generated the light, and the sight of her room, flooded with radiance and studded with electric buttons, revived her. There were buttons and switches everywhere—buttons to call for food, for music, for clothing. There was the hot-bath button, by pressure of which a basin of (imitation) marble rose out of the floor, filled to the brim with a warm deodorized liquid. There was the cold-bath button. There was the button that produced literature. And there were of course the buttons by which she communicated with her friends. The room, though it contained nothing, was in touch with all that she cared for in the world.

Vashti's next move was to turn off the isolation switch, and all the accumulations of the last three minutes burst upon her. The room was filled with the noise of bells, and speaking-tubes. What was the new food like? Could she recommend it? Has she had any ideas lately? Might one tell her one's own ideas? Would she make an engagement to visit the public nurseries at an early date?—say this day month.

To most of these questions she replied with irritation—a growing quality in that accelerated age. She said that the new food was horrible. That she could not visit the public nurseries through press of engagements. That she had no ideas of her own but had just been told one—that four stars and three in the middle were like a man: she doubted there was much in it. Then she switched off her correspondents, for it was time to deliver her lecture on Australian music.

The clumsy system of public gatherings had been long since abandoned; neither Vashti nor her audience stirred from their rooms. Seated in her armchair she spoke, while they in their armchairs heard her, fairly well, and saw her, fairly well. She opened with a humorous account of music in the pre-Mongolian epoch, and went on to describe the great outburst of song that followed the Chinese conquest. Remote and primæval as were the methods of I-San-So and the Brisbane school, she yet felt (she said) that study of them might repay the musicians of today: they had freshness; they had, above all, ideas. Her lecture, which lasted ten minutes, was well received, and at its conclusion she and many of her audience listened to a lecture on the sea; there were ideas to be got from the sea; the speaker had donned a respirator and visited it lately. Then she fed, talked to many friends, had a bath, talked again, and summoned her bed.

The bed was not to her liking. It was too large, and she had a feeling for a small bed. Complaint was useless, for beds were of the same dimension all over the world, and to have had an alternative size would have involved vast alterations in the Machine. Vashti isolated herself—it was necessary, for neither day nor night existed under the ground—and reviewed all that had happened since she had summoned the bed last. Ideas? Scarcely any. Events—was Kuno's invitation an event?

By her side, on the little reading-desk, was a survival from the ages of litter—one book. This was the Book of the Machine. In it were instructions against every possible contingency. If she was hot or cold or dyspeptic or at a loss for a word, she went to the Book, and it told her which button to press. The Central Committee published it. In accordance with a growing habit, it was richly bound.

Sitting up in the bed, she took it reverently in her hands. She glanced round the glowing room as if some one might be watching her. Then, half ashamed, half joyful, she murmured, "O Machine!" and raised the volume to her lips. Thrice she kissed it, thrice inclined her head, thrice she felt the delirium of acquiescence. Her ritual performed, she turned to page 1367, which gave the times of the departure of the air-ships from the island in the southern hemisphere, under whose soil she lived, to the island in the northern hemisphere, whereunder lived her son.

She thought, "I have not the time."

She made the room dark and slept; she awoke and made the room light; she ate and exchanged ideas with her friends, and listened to music and attended lectures; she made the room dark and slept. Above her, beneath her, and around her, the Machine hummed eternally; she did not notice the noise, for she had been born with it in her ears. The earth, carrying her, hummed as it sped through silence, turning her now to the invisible sun, now to the invisible stars. She awoke and made the room light.

"Kuno!"

"I will not talk to you," he answered, "until you come."

"Have you been on the surface of the earth since we spoke last?"

His image faded.

Again she consulted the Book. She became very nervous and lay back in her chair palpitating. Think of her as without teeth or hair. Presently she directed the chair to the wall, and pressed an unfamiliar button. The wall swung apart slowly. Through the opening she saw a tunnel that curved slightly, so that its goal was not visible. Should she go to see her son, here was the beginning of the journey.

Of course she knew all about the communication-system. There was nothing mysterious in it. She would summon a car and it would fly with her down the tunnel until it reached the lift that communicated with the air-ship station: the system had been in use for many, many years, long before the universal establishment of the Machine. And of course she had studied the civilization that had immediately preceded her own—the civilization that had mistaken the functions of the system, and had used it for bringing people to things, instead of for bringing things to people. Those funny old days, when men went for change of air instead of changing the air in their rooms! And yet—she was frightened of the tunnel: she had not seen it since her last child was born. It curved—but not quite as she remembered; it was brilliant—but not quite as brilliant as a lecturer had suggested. Vashti was seized with the terrors of direct experience. She shrank back into the room, and the wall closed up again.

"Kuno," she said, "I cannot come to see you. I am not well."

Immediately an enormous apparatus fell on to her out of the ceiling, a thermometer was automatically laid upon her heart. She lay powerless. Cool pads soothed her forehead. Kuno had telegraphed to her doctor.

So the human passions still blundered up and down in the Machine. Vashti drank the medicine that the doctor projected into her mouth, and the machinery retired into the ceiling. The voice of Kuno was heard asking how she felt.

"Better." Then with irritation: "But why do you not come to me instead?"

"Because I cannot leave this place."

"Why?"

"Because, any moment, something tremendous many happen."

"Have you been on the surface of the earth yet?"

"Not yet."

"Then what is it?"

"I will not tell you through the Machine."

She resumed her life.

But she thought of Kuno as a baby, his birth, his removal to the public nurseries, her own visit to him there, his visits to her—visits which stopped when the Machine had assigned him a room on the other side of the earth. "Parents, duties of," said the Book of the Machine, "cease at the moment of birth. P.422327483." True, but there was something special about Kuno—indeed there had been something special about all her children—and, after all, she must brave the journey if he desired it. And "something tremendous might happen." What did that mean? The nonsense of a youthful man, no doubt, but she must go. Again she pressed the unfamiliar button, again the wall swung back, and she saw the tunnel that curves out of sight. Clasping the Book, she rose, tottered on to the platform, and summoned the car. Her room closed behind her: the journey to the northern hemisphere had begun.

Of course it was perfectly easy. The car approached and in it she found armchairs exactly like her own. When she signaled, it stopped, and she tottered into the lift. One other passenger was in the lift, the first fellow creature she had seen face to face for months. Few travelled in these days, for, thanks to the advance of science, the earth was exactly alike all over. Rapid intercourse, from which the previous civilization had hoped so much, had ended by defeating itself. What was the good of going to Peking when it was just like Shrewsbury? Why return to Shrewsbury when it would all be like Peking? Men seldom moved their bodies; all unrest was concentrated in the soul.

The air-ship service was a relic from the former age. It was kept up, because it was easier to keep it up than to stop it or to diminish it, but it now far exceeded the wants of the population. Vessel after vessel would rise from the vomitories of Rye or of Christchurch (I use the antique names), would sail into the crowded sky, and would draw up at the wharves of the south—empty. So nicely adjusted was the system, so independent of meteorology, that the sky, whether calm or cloudy, resembled a vast kaleidoscope whereon the same patterns periodically recurred. The ship on which Vashti sailed started now at sunset, now at dawn. But always, as it passed above Rheims, it would neighbour the ship that served between Helsingfors and the Brazils, and, every third time it surmounted the Alps, the fleet of Palermo would cross its track behind. Night and day, wind and storm, tide and earthquake, impeded man no longer. He had harnessed Leviathan. All the old literature, with its praise of Nature, and its fear of Nature, rang false as the prattle of a child.

Yet as Vashti saw the vast flank of the ship, stained with exposure to the outer air, her horror of direct experience returned. It was not quite like the air-ship in the cinematophote. For one thing it smelt—not strongly or unpleasantly, but it did smell, and with her eyes shut she should have known that a new thing was close to her. Then she had to walk to it from the lift, had to submit to glances from the other passengers. The man in front dropped his Book—no great matter, but it disquieted them all. In the rooms, if the Book was dropped, the floor raised it mechanically, but the gangway to the air-ship was not so prepared, and the sacred volume lay motionless. They stopped—the thing was unforeseen—and the man, instead of picking up his property, felt the muscles of his arm to see how they had failed him. Then some one actually said with direct utterance: "We shall be late"—and they trooped on board, Vashti treading on the pages as she did so.

Inside, her anxiety increased. The arrangements were old-fashioned and rough. There was even a female attendant, to whom she would have to announce her wants during the voyage. Of course a revolving platform ran the length of the boat, but she was expected to walk from it to her cabin. Some cabins were better than others, and she did not get the best. She thought the attendant had been unfair, and spasms of rage shook her. The glass valves had closed, she could not go back. She saw, at the end of the vestibule, the lift in which she had ascended going quietly up and down, empty. Beneath those corridors of shining tiles were rooms, tier below tier, reaching far into the earth, and in each room there sat a human being, eating, or sleeping, or producing ideas. And buried deep in the hive was her own room. Vashti was afraid.

"O Machine! O Machine!" she murmured, and caressed her Book, and was comforted.

Then the sides of the vestibule seemed to melt together, as do the passages that we see in dreams, the lift vanished, the Book that had been dropped slid to the left and vanished, polished tiles rushed by like a stream of water, there was a slight jar, and the air-ship, issuing from its tunnel, soared above the waters of a tropical ocean.

It was night. For a moment she saw the coast of Sumatra edged by the phosphorescence of waves, and crowned by lighthouses, still sending forth their disregarded beams. These also vanished, and only the stars distracted her. They were not motionless, but swayed to and fro above her head, thronging out of one sky-light into another, as if the universe and not the air-ship was careening. And, as often happens on clear nights, they seemed now to be in perspective, now on a plane; now piled tier beyond tier into the infinite heavens, now concealing infinity, a roof limiting for ever the visions of men. In either case they seemed intolerable. "Are we to travel in the dark?" called the passengers angrily, and the attendant, who had been careless, generated the light, and pulled down the blinds of pliable metal. When the air-ships had been built, the desire to look direct at things still lingered in the world. Hence the extraordinary number of skylights and windows, and the proportionate discomfort to those who were civilized and refined. Even in Vashti's cabin one star peeped through a flaw in the blind, and after a few hours' uneasy slumber, she was disturbed by an unfamiliar glow, which was the dawn.

Quick as the ship had sped westwards, the earth had rolled eastwards quicker still, and had dragged back Vashti and her companions towards the sun. Science could prolong the night, but only for a little, and those high hopes of neutralizing the earth's diurnal revolution had passed, together with hopes that were possibly higher. To "keep pace with the sun," or even to outstrip it, had been the aim of the civilization preceding this. Racing aeroplanes had been built for the purpose, capable of enormous speed, and steered by the greatest intellects of the epoch. Round the globe they went, round and round, westward, westward, round and round, amidst humanity's applause. In vain. The globe went eastward quicker still, horrible accidents occurred, and the Committee of the Machine, at the time rising into prominence, declared the pursuit illegal, unmechanical, and punishable by Homelessness.

Of Homelessness more will be said later.

Doubtless the Committee was right. Yet the attempt to "defeat the sun" aroused the last common interest that our race experienced about the heavenly bodies, or indeed about anything. It was the last time that men were compacted by thinking of a power outside the world. The sun had conquered, yet it was the end of his spiritual dominion. Dawn, midday, twilight, the zodiacal path, touched neither men's lives not their hearts, and science retreated into the ground, to concentrate herself upon problems that she was certain of solving.

So when Vashti found her cabin invaded by a rosy finger of light, she was annoyed, and tried to adjust the blind. But the blind flew up altogether, and she saw through the skylight small pink clouds, swaying against a background of blue, and as the sun crept higher, its radiance entered direct, brimming down the wall, like a golden sea. It rose and fell with the air-ship's motion, just as waves rise and fall, but it advanced steadily, as a tide advances. Unless she was careful, it would strike her face. A spasm of horror shook her and she rang for the attendant. The attendant too was horrified, but she could do nothing; it was not her place to mend the blind. She could only suggest that the lady should change her cabin, which she accordingly prepared to do.

People were almost exactly alike all over the world, but the attendant of the air-ship, perhaps owing to her exceptional duties, had grown a little out of the common. She had often to address passengers with direct speech, and this had given her a certain roughness and originality of manner. When Vashti swerved away from the sunbeams with a cry, she behaved barbarically—she put out her hand to steady her.

"How dare you!" exclaimed the passenger. "You forget yourself!"

The woman was confused, and apologized for not having let her fall. People never touched one another. The custom had become obsolete, owing to the Machine.

"Where are we now?" asked Vashti haughtily.

"We are over Asia," said the attendant, anxious to be polite.

"Asia?"

"You must excuse my common way of speaking. I have got into the habit of calling places over which I pass by their unmechanical names."

"Oh, I remember Asia. The Mongols came from it."

"Beneath us, in the open air, stood a city that was once called Simla."

"Have you ever heard of the Mongols and of the Brisbane school?"

"No."

"Brisbane also stood in the open air."

"Those mountains to the right—let me show you them." She pushed back a metal blind. The main chain of the Himalayas was revealed. "They were once called the Roof of the World, those mountains."

"You must remember that, before the dawn of civilization, they seemed to be an impenetrable wall that touched the stars. It was supposed that no one but the gods could exist above their summits. How we have advanced, thanks to the Machine!"

"How we have advanced, thanks to the Machine!" said Vashti.

"How we have advanced, thanks to the Machine!" echoed the passenger who had dropped his Book the night before, and who was standing in the passage.

"And that white stuff in the cracks?—what is it?"

"I have forgotten its name."

"Cover the window, please. These mountains give me no ideas."

The northern aspect of the Himalayas was in deep shadow: on the Indian slope the sun had just prevailed. The forests had been destroyed during the literature epoch for the purpose of making newspaper-pulp, but the snows were awakening to their morning glory, and clouds still hung on the breasts of Kinchinjunga. In the plain were seen the ruins of cities, with diminished rivers creeping by their walls, and by the sides of these were sometimes the signs of vomitories, marking the cities of today. Over the whole prospect air-ships rushed, crossing the inter-crossing with incredible aplomb, and rising nonchalantly when they desired to escape the perturbations of the lower atmosphere and to traverse the Roof of the World.

"We have indeed advanced, thanks to the Machine," repeated the attendant, and hid the Himalayas behind a metal blind.

The day dragged wearily forward. The passengers sat each in his cabin, avoiding one another with an almost physical repulsion and longing to be once more under the surface of the earth. There were eight or ten of them, mostly young males, sent out from the public nurseries to inhabit the rooms of those who had died in various parts of the earth. The man who had dropped his Book was on the homeward journey. He had been sent to Sumatra for the purpose of propagating the race. Vashti alone was travelling by her private will.

At midday she took a second glance at the earth. The air-ship was crossing another range of mountains, but she could see little, owing to clouds. Masses of black rock hovered below her, and merged indistinctly into grey. Their shapes were fantastic; one of them resembled a prostrate man.

"No ideas here," murmured Vashti, and hid the Caucasus behind a metal blind.

In the evening she looked again. They were crossing a golden sea, in which lay many small islands and one peninsula. She repeated, "No ideas here," and hid Greece behind a metal blind.

Part II: The Mending Apparatus

By a vestibule, by a lift, by a tubular railway, by a platform, by a sliding door—by reversing all the steps of her departure did Vashti arrive at her son's room, which exactly resembled her own. She might well declare that the visit was superfluous. The buttons, the knobs, the reading-desk with the Book, the temperature, the atmosphere, the illumination—all were exactly the same. And if Kuno himself, flesh of her flesh, stood close beside her at last, what profit was there in that? She was too well-bred to shake him by the hand.

Averting her eyes, she spoke as follows:

"Here I am. I have had the most terrible journey and greatly retarded the development of my soul. It is not worth it, Kuno, it is not worth it. My time is too precious. The sunlight almost touched me, and I have met with the rudest people. I can only stop a few minutes. Say what you want to say, and then I must return."

"I have been threatened with Homelessness," said Kuno.

She looked at him now.

"I have been threatened with Homelessness, and I could not tell you such a thing through the Machine."

Homelessness means death. The victim is exposed to the air, which kills him.

"I have been outside since I spoke to you last. The tremendous thing has happened, and they have discovered me."

"But why shouldn't you go outside?" she exclaimed. "It is perfectly legal, perfectly mechanical, to visit the surface of the earth. I have lately been to a lecture on the sea; there is no objection to that; one simply summons a respirator and gets an Egression-permit. It is not the kind of thing that spiritually minded people do, and I begged you not to do it, but there is no legal objection to it."

"I did not get an Egression-permit."

"Then how did you get out?"

"I found out a way of my own."

The phrase conveyed no meaning to her, and he had to repeat it.

"A way of your own?" she whispered. "But that would be wrong."

"Why?"

The question shocked her beyond measure.

"You are beginning to worship the Machine," he said coldly. "You think it irreligious of me to have found out a way of my own. It was just what the Committee thought, when they threatened me with Homelessness."

At this she grew angry. "I worship nothing!" she cried. "I am most advanced. I don't think you irreligious, for there is no such thing as religion left. All the fear and the superstition that existed once have been destroyed by the Machine. I only meant that to find out a way of your own was——Besides, there is no new way out."

"So it is always supposed."

"Except through the vomitories, for which one must have an Egression-permit, it is impossible to get out. The Book says so."

"Well, the Book's wrong, for I have been out on my feet."

For Kuno was possessed of a certain physical strength.

By these days it was a demerit to be muscular. Each infant was examined at birth, and all who promised undue strength were destroyed. Humanitarians may protest, but it would have been no true kindness to let an athlete live; he would never have been happy in that state of life to which the Machine had called him; he would have yearned for trees to climb, rivers to bathe in, meadows and hills against which he might measure his body. Man must be adapted to his surroundings, must he not? In the dawn of the world our weakly must be exposed on Mount Taygetus, in its twilight our strong will suffer euthanasia, that the Machine may progress, that the Machine may progress, that the Machine may progress eternally.

"You know that we have lost the sense of space. We say 'space is annihilated,' but we have annihilated not space, but the sense thereof. We have lost a part of ourselves. I determined to recover it, and I began by walking up and down the platform of the railway outside my room. Up and down, until I was tired, and so did recapture the meaning of 'Near' and 'Far.' 'Near' is a place to which I can get quickly on my feet, not a place to which the train or the air-ship will take me quickly. 'Far' is a place to which I cannot get quickly on my feet; the vomitory is 'far,' though I could be there in thirty-eight seconds by summoning the train. Man is the measure. That was my first lesson. Man's feet are the measure for distance, his hands are the measure for ownership, his body is the measure for all that is lovable and desirable and strong. Then I went further: it was then that I called to you for the first time, and you would not come.

"This city, as you know, is built deep beneath the surface of the earth, with only the vomitories protruding. Having paced the platform outside my own room, I took the lift to the next platform and paced that also, and so with each in turn, until I came to the topmost, above which begins the earth. All the platforms were exactly alike, and all that I gained by visiting them was to develop my sense of space and my muscles. I think I should have been content with this—it is not a little thing—but as I walked and brooded, it occurred to me that our cities had been built in the days when men still breathed the outer air, and that there had been ventilation shafts for the workmen. I could think of nothing but these ventilation shafts. Had they been destroyed by all the food-tubes and medicine-tubes and music tubes that the Machine has evolved lately? Or did traces of them remain? One thing was certain. If I came upon them anywhere, it would be in the railway-tunnels of the topmost story. Everywhere else, all space was accounted for.

"I am telling my story quickly, but don't think that I was not a coward or that your answers never depressed me. It is not the proper thing, it is not mechanical, it is not decent to walk along a railway-tunnel. I did not fear that I might tread upon a live rail and be killed. I feared something far more intangible—doing what was not contemplated by the Machine. Then I said to myself, 'Man is the measure,' and I went, and after many visits I found an opening.

"The tunnels, of course, were lighted. Everything is light, artificial light; darkness is the exception. So when I saw a black gap in the tiles, I knew that it was an exception, and rejoiced. I put in my arm—I could put in no more at first—and waved it round and round in ecstasy. I loosened another tile, and put in my head, and shouted into the darkness: 'I am coming, I shall do it yet,' and my voice reverberated down endless passages. I seemed to hear the spirits of those dead workmen who had returned each evening to the starlight and to their wives, and all the generations who had lived in the open air called back to me, 'You will do it yet, you are coming.'"

He paused, and, absurd as he was, his last words moved her. For Kuno had lately asked to be a father, and his request had been refused by the Committee. His was not a type that the Machine desired to hand on.

"Then a train passed. It brushed by me, but I thrust my head and arms into the hole. I had done enough for one day, so I crawled back to the platform, went down in the lift, and summoned my bed. Ah, what dreams! And again I called you, and again you refused."

She shook her head and said:

"Don't. Don't talk of these terrible things. You make me miserable. You are throwing civilization away."

"But I had got back the sense of space, and a man cannot rest then. I determined to get in at the hole and climb the shaft. And so I exercised my arms. Day after day I went through ridiculous movements, until my flesh ached, and I could hang by my hands and hold the pillow of my bed outstretched for many minutes. Then I summoned a respirator, and started.

"It was easy at first. The mortar had somehow rotted, and I soon pushed some more tiles in, and clambered after them into the darkness, and the spirits of the dead comforted me. I don't know what I mean by that. I just say what I felt. I felt, for the first time, that a protest had been lodged against corruption, and that even as the dead were comforting me, so I was comforting the unborn. I felt that humanity existed, and that it existed without clothes. How can I possibly explain this? It was naked, humanity seemed naked, and all these tubes and buttons and machineries neither came into the world with us, nor will they follow us out, nor do they matter supremely while we are here. Had I been strong, I would have torn off every garment I had, and gone out into the outer air unswaddled. But this is not for me, nor perhaps for my generation. I climbed with my respirator and my hygienic clothes and my dietetic tabloids! Better thus than not at all.

"There was a ladder, made of some primæval metal. The light from the railway fell upon its lowest rungs, and I saw that it led straight upwards out of the rubble at the bottom of the shaft. Perhaps our ancestors ran up and down it a dozen times daily, in their building. As I climbed, the rough edges cut through my gloves so that my hands bled. The light helped me for a little, and then came darkness and, worse still, silence which pierced my ears like a sword. The Machine hums! Did you know that? Its hum penetrates our blood, and may even guide our thoughts. Who knows! I was getting beyond its power. Then I thought: 'This silence means that I am doing wrong.' But I heard voices in the silence, and again they strengthened me." He laughed. "I had need of them. The next moment I cracked my head against something."

She sighed.

"I had reached one of those pneumatic stoppers that defend us from the outer air. You may have noticed them on the air-ship. Pitch dark, my feet on the rungs of an invisible ladder, my hands cut; I cannot explain how I lived through this part, but the voices still comforted me, and I felt for fastenings. The stopper, I suppose, was about eight feet across. I passed my hand over it as far as I could reach. It was perfectly smooth. I felt it almost to the centre. Not quite to the centre, for my arm was too short. Then the voice said: 'Jump. It is worth it. There may be a handle in the centre, and you may catch hold of it and so come to us your own way. And if there is no handle, so that you may fall and are dashed to pieces—it is still worth it: you will still come to us your own way.' So I jumped. There was a handle, and—"

He paused. Tears gathered in his mother's eyes. She knew that he was fated. If he did not die today he would die tomorrow. There was not room for such a person in the world. And with her pity disgust mingled. She was ashamed at having borne such a son, she who had always been so respectable and so full of ideas. Was he really the little boy to whom she had taught the use of his stops and buttons, and to whom she had given his first lessons in the Book? The very hair that disfigured his lip showed that he was reverting to some savage type. On atavism the Machine can have no mercy.

"There was a handle, and I did catch it. I hung tranced over the darkness and heard the hum of these workings as the last whisper in a dying dream. All the things I had cared about and all the people I had spoken to through tubes appeared infinitely little. Meanwhile the handle revolved. My weight had set something in motion and I spun slowly, and then—

"I cannot describe it. I was lying with my face to the sunshine. Blood poured from my nose and ears and I heard a tremendous roaring. The stopper, with me clinging to it, had simply been blown out of the earth, and the air that we make down here was escaping through the vent into the air above. It burst up like a fountain. I crawled back to it—for the upper air hurts—and, as it were, I took great sips from the edge. My respirator had flown goodness knows where, my clothes were torn. I just lay with my lips close to the hole, and I sipped until the bleeding stopped. You can imagine nothing so curious. This hollow in the grass—I will speak of it in a minute—the sun shining into it, not brilliantly but through marbled clouds—the peace, the nonchalance, the sense of space, and, brushing my cheek, the roaring fountain of our artificial air! Soon I spied my respirator, bobbing up and down in the current high above my head, and higher still were many air-ships. But no one ever looks out of air-ships, and in any case they could not have picked me up. There I was, stranded. The sun shone a little way down the shaft, and revealed the topmost rung of the ladder, but it was hopeless trying to reach it. I should either have been tossed up again by the escape, or else have fallen in, and died. I could only lie on the grass, sipping and sipping, and from time to time glancing around me.

"I knew that I was in Wessex, for I had taken care to go to a lecture on the subject before starting. Wessex lies above the room in which we are talking now. It was once an important state. Its kings held all the southern coast from the Andredswald to Cornwall, while the Wansdyke protected them on the north, running over the high ground. The lecturer was only concerned with the rise of Wessex, so I do not know how long it remained an international power, nor would the knowledge have assisted me. To tell the truth I could do nothing but laugh, during this part. There was I, with a pneumatic stopper by my side and a respirator bobbing over my head, imprisoned, all three of us, in a grass-grown hollow that was edged with fern."

Then he grew grave again.

"Lucky for me that it was a hollow. For the air began to fall back into it and to fill it as water fills a bowl. I could crawl about. Presently I stood. I breathed a mixture, in which the air that hurts predominated whenever I tried to climb the sides. This was not so bad. I had not lost my tabloids and remained ridiculously cheerful, and as for the Machine, I forgot about it altogether. My one aim now was to get to the top, where the ferns were, and to view whatever objects lay beyond.

"I rushed the slope. The new air was still too bitter for me and I came rolling back, after a momentary vision of something grey. The sun grew very feeble, and I remembered that he was in Scorpio—I had been to a lecture on that too. If the sun is in Scorpio, and you are in Wessex, it means that you must be as quick as you can, or it will get too dark. (This is the first bit of useful information I have ever got from a lecture, and I expect it will be the last.) It made me try frantically to breathe the new air, and to advance as far as I dared out of my pond. The hollow filled so slowly. At times I thought that the fountain played with less vigour. My respirator seemed to dance nearer the earth; the roar was decreasing."

He broke off.

"I don't think this is interesting you. The rest will interest you even less. There are no ideas in it, and I wish that I had not troubled you to come. We are too different, mother."

She told him to continue.

"It was evening before I climbed the bank. The sun had very nearly slipped out of the sky by this time, and I could not get a good view. You, who have just crossed the Roof of the World, will not want to hear an account of the little hills that I saw—low colourless hills. But to me they were living and the turf that covered them was a skin, under which their muscles rippled, and I felt that those hills had called with incalculable force to men in the past, and that men had loved them. Now they sleep—perhaps for ever. They commune with humanity in dreams. Happy the man, happy the woman, who awakes the hills of Wessex. For though they sleep, they will never die."

His voice rose passionately.

"Cannot you see, cannot all you lecturers see, that it is we that are dying, and that down here the only thing that really lives is the Machine? We created the Machine, to do our will, but we cannot make it do our will now. It has robbed us of the sense of space and of the sense of touch, it has blurred every human relation and narrowed down love to a carnal act, it has paralysed our bodies and our wills, and now it compels us to worship it. The Machine develops—but not on our lines. The Machine proceeds—but not to our goal. We only exist as the blood corpuscles that course through its arteries, and if it could work without us, it would let us die. Oh, I have no remedy—or, at least, only one—to tell men again and again that I have seen the hills of Wessex as Ælfrid saw them when he overthrew the Danes.

"So the sun set. I forgot to mention that a belt of mist lay between my hill and other hills, and that it was the colour of pearl."

He broke off for the second time.

"Go on," said his mother wearily.

He shook his head.

"Go on. Nothing that you say can distress me now. I am hardened."

"I had meant to tell you the rest, but I cannot: I know that I cannot: good-bye."

Vashti stood irresolute. All her nerves were tingling with his blasphemies. But she was also inquisitive.

"This is unfair," she complained. "You have called me across the world to hear your story, and hear it I will. Tell me—as briefly as possible, for this is a disastrous waste of time—tell me how you returned to civilization."

"Oh—that!" he said, starting. "You would like to hear about civilization. Certainly. Had I got to where my respirator fell down?"

"No—but I understand everything now. You put on your respirator, and managed to walk along the surface of the earth to a vomitory, and there your conduct was reported to the Central Committee."

"By no means."

He passed his hand over his forehead, as if dispelling some strong impression. Then, resuming his narrative, he warmed to it again.

"My respirator fell about sunset. I had mentioned that the fountain seemed feebler, had I not?"

"Yes."

"About sunset, it let the respirator fall. As I said, I had entirely forgotten about the Machine, and I paid no great attention at the time, being occupied with other things. I had my pool of air, into which I could dip when the outer keenness became intolerable, and which would possibly remain for days, provided that no wind sprang up to disperse it. Not until it was too late did I realize what the stoppage of the escape implied. You see—the gap in the tunnel had been mended; the Mending Apparatus; the Mending Apparatus, was after me.

"One other warning I had, but I neglected it. The sky at night was clearer than it had been in the day, and the moon, which was about half the sky behind the sun, shone into the dell at moments quite brightly. I was in my usual place—on the boundary between the two atmospheres—when I thought I saw something dark move across the bottom of the dell, and vanish into the shaft. In my folly, I ran down. I bent over and listened, and I thought I heard a faint scraping noise in the depths.

"At this—but it was too late—I took alarm. I determined to put on my respirator and to walk right out of the dell. But my respirator had gone. I knew exactly where it had fallen—between the stopper and the aperture—and I could even feel the mark that it had made in the turf. It had gone, and I realized that something evil was at work, and I had better escape to the other air, and, if I must die, die running towards the cloud that had been the colour of a pearl. I never started. Out of the shaft—it is too horrible. A worm, a long white worm, had crawled out of the shaft and was gliding over the moonlit grass.

"I screamed. I did everything that I should not have done, I stamped upon the creature instead of flying from it, and it at once curled round the ankle. Then we fought. The worm let me run all over the dell, but edged up my leg as I ran. 'Help!' I cried. (That part is too awful. It belongs to the part that you will never know.) 'Help!' I cried. (Why cannot we suffer in silence?) 'Help!' I cried. Then my feet were wound together, I fell, I was dragged away from the dear ferns and the living hills, and past the great metal stopper (I can tell you this part), and I thought it might save me again if I caught hold of the handle. It also was enwrapped, it also. Oh, the whole dell was full of the things. They were searching it in all directions, they were denuding it, and the white snouts of others peeped out of the hole, ready if needed. Everything that could be moved they brought—brushwood, bundles of fern, everything, and down we all went intertwined into hell. The last things that I saw, ere the stopper closed after us, were certain stars, and I felt that a man of my sort lived in the sky. For I did fight, I fought till the very end, and it was only my head hitting against the ladder that quieted me. I woke up in this room. The worms had vanished. I was surrounded by artificial air, artificial light, artificial peace, and my friends were calling to me down speaking-tubes to know whether I had come across any new ideas lately."

Here his story ended. Discussion of it was impossible, and Vashti turned to go.

"It will end in Homelessness," she said quietly.

"I wish it would," retorted Kuno.

"The Machine has been most merciful."

"I prefer the mercy of God."

"By that superstitious phrase, do you mean that you could live in the outer air?"

"Yes."

"Have you ever seen, round the vomitories, the bones of those who were extruded after the Great Rebellion?"

"Yes."

"They were left where they perished for our edification. A few crawled away, but they perished, too—who can doubt it? And so with the Homeless of our own day. The surface of the earth supports life no longer."

"Indeed."

"Ferns and a little grass may survive, but all higher forms have perished. Has any air-ship detected them?"

"No."

"Has any lecturer dealt with them?"

"No."

"Then why this obstinacy?"

"Because I have seen them," he exploded.

"Seen *what*?"

"Because I have seen her in the twilight—because she came to my help when I called—because she, too, was entangled by the worms, and, luckier than I, was killed by one of them piercing her throat."

He was mad. Vashti departed, nor, in the troubles that followed, did she ever see his face again.

Part III: The Homeless

During the years that followed Kuno's escapade, two important developments took place in the Machine. On the surface they were revolutionary, but in either case men's minds had been prepared beforehand, and they did but express tendencies that were latent already.

The first of these was the abolition of respirators.

Advanced thinkers, like Vashti, had always held it foolish to visit the surface of the earth. Air-ships might be necessary, but what was the good of going out for mere curiosity and crawling along for a mile or two in a terrestrial motor? The habit was vulgar and perhaps faintly improper: it was unproductive of ideas, and had no connection with the habits that really mattered. So respirators were abolished, and with them, of course, the terrestrial motors, and except for a few lecturers, who complained that they were debarred access to their subject-matter, the development was accepted quietly. Those who still wanted to know what the earth was like had after all only to listen to some gramophone, or to look into some cinematophote. And even the lecturers acquiesced when they found that a lecture on the sea was none the less stimulating when compiled out of other lectures that had already been delivered on the same subject. "Beware of first-hand ideas!" exclaimed one of the most advanced of them. "First-hand ideas do not really exist. They are but the physical impressions produced by life and fear, and on this gross foundation who could erect a philosophy? Let your ideas be second-hand, and if possible tenth-hand, for then they will be far removed from that disturbing element—direct observation. Do not learn anything about this subject of mine—the French Revolution. Learn instead what I think that Enicharmon thought Urizen thought Gutch thought Ho-Yung thought Chi-Bo-Sing thought Lafcadio Hearn thought Carlyle thought Mirabeau said about the French Revolution. Through the medium of these eight great minds, the blood that was shed at Paris and the windows that were broken at Versailles will be clarified to an idea which you may employ most profitably in your daily lives. But be sure that the intermediates are many and varied, for in history one authority exists to counteract another. Urizen must counteract the scepticism of Ho-Yung and Enicharmon, I must myself counteract the impetuosity of Gutch. You who listen to me are in a better position to judge about the French Revolution than I am.

Your descendants will be even in a better position than you, for they will learn what you think I think, and yet another intermediate will be added to the chain. And in time"—his voice rose—"there will come a generation that has got beyond facts, beyond impressions, a generation absolutely colourless, a generation

'seraphically free

From taint of personality,'

which will see the French Revolution not as it happened, nor as they would like it to have happened, but as it would have happened, had it taken place in the days of the Machine."

Tremendous applause greeted this lecture, which did but voice a feeling already latent in the minds of men—a feeling that terrestrial facts must be ignored, and that the abolition of respirators was a positive gain. It was even suggested that air-ships should be abolished too. This was not done, because air-ships had somehow worked themselves into the Machine's system. But year by year they were used less, and mentioned less by thoughtful men.

The second great development was the re-establishment of religion.

This, too, had been voiced in the celebrated lecture. No one could mistake the reverent tone in which the peroration had concluded, and it awakened a responsive echo in the heart of each. Those who had long worshipped silently, now began to talk. They described the strange feeling of peace that came over them when they handled the Book of the Machine, the pleasure that it was to repeat certain numerals out of it, however little meaning those numerals conveyed to the outward ear, the ecstasy of touching a button, however unimportant, or of ringing an electric bell, however superfluously.

"The Machine," they exclaimed, "feeds us and clothes us and houses us; through it we speak to one another, through it we see one another, in it we have our being. The Machine is the friend of ideas and the enemy of superstition; the Machine is omnipotent, eternal; blessed is the Machine." And before long this allocution was printed on the first page of the Book, and in subsequent editions the ritual swelled into a complicated system of praise and prayer. The word "religion" was sedulously avoided, and in theory the Machine was still the creation and the implement of man. But in practice all, save a few retrogrades, worshipped it as divine. Nor was it worshipped in unity. One believer would be chiefly impressed by the blue optic plates, through which he saw other believers; another by the mending apparatus, which sinful Kuno had compared to worms; another by the lifts, another by the Book. And each would pray to this or to that, and ask it to intercede for him with the Machine as a whole. Persecution—that also was present. It did not break out, for reasons that will be set forward shortly. But it was latent, and all who did not accept the minimum known as "undenominational Mechanism" lived in danger of Homelessness, which means death, as we know.

To attribute these two great developments to the Central Committee, is to take a very narrow view of civilization.

The Central Committee announced the developments, it is true, but they were no more the cause of them than were the kings of the imperialistic period the cause of war. Rather did they yield to some invincible pressure, which came no one knew whither, and which, when gratified, was succeeded by some new pressure equally invincible. To such a state of affairs it is convenient to give the name of progress. No one confessed the Machine was out of hand. Year by year it was served with increased efficiency and decreased intelligence. The better a man knew his own duties upon it, the less he understood the duties of his neighbour, and in all the world there was not one who understood the monster as a whole. Those master brains had perished. They had left full directions, it is true, and their successors had each of them mastered a portion of those directions. But Humanity, in its desire for comfort, had over-reached itself. It had exploited the riches of nature too far. Quietly and complacently, it was sinking into decadence, and progress had come to mean the progress of the Machine.

As for Vashti, her life went peacefully forward until the final disaster. She made her room dark and slept; she awoke and made the room light. She lectured and attended lectures. She exchanged ideas with her innumerable friends and believed she was growing more spiritual. At times a friend was granted Euthanasia, and left his or her room for the Homelessness that is beyond all human conception. Vashti did not much mind. After an unsuccessful lecture, she would sometimes ask for Euthanasia herself. But the death-rate was not permitted to exceed the birth-rate, and the Machine had hitherto refused it to her.

The troubles began quietly, long before she was conscious of them.

One day she was astonished at receiving a message from her son. They never communicated, having nothing in common, and she had only heard indirectly that he was still alive, and had been transferred from the northern hemisphere, where he had behaved so mischievously, to the southern—indeed, to a room not far from her own.

"Does he want me to visit him?" she thought. "Never again, never. And I have not the time."

No, it was madness of another kind.

He refused to visualize his face upon the blue plate, and speaking out of the darkness with solemnity said:

"The Machine stops."

"What do you say?"

"The Machine is stopping, I know it. I know the signs."

She burst into a peal of laughter. He heard her and was angry, and they spoke no more.

"Can you imagine anything more absurd?" she cried to a friend. "A man who was my son believes that the Machine is stopping. It would be impious if it was not mad."

"The Machine is stopping?" her friend replied. "What does that mean? The phrase conveys nothing to me."

"Nor to me."

"He does not refer, I suppose, to the trouble there has been lately with the music?"

"Oh no, of course not. Let us talk about music."

"Have you complained to the authorities?"

"Yes, and they say it wants mending, and referred me to the Committee of the Mending Apparatus. I complained of those curious gasping sighs that disfigure the symphonies of the Brisbane school. They sound like some one in pain. The Committee of the Mending Apparatus say that it shall be remedied shortly."

Obscurely worried, she resumed her life. For one thing, the defect in the music irritated her. For another thing, she could not forget Kuno's speech. If he had known that the music was out of repair—he could not know it, for he detested music—if he had known that it was wrong, "the Machine stops" was exactly the venomous sort of remark he would have made. Of course he had made it at a venture, but the coincidence annoyed her, and she spoke with some petulance to the Committee of the Mending Apparatus.

They replied, as before, that the defect would be set right shortly.

"Shortly? At once!" she retorted. "Why should I be worried by imperfect music? Things are always put right at once. If you do not mend it at once, I shall complain to the Central Committee."

"No personal complaints are received by the Central Committee," the Committee of the Mending Apparatus replied.

"Through whom am I to make my complaint, then?"

"Through us."

"I complain then."

"Your complaint shall be forwarded in its turn."

"Have others complained?"

This question was unmechanical, and the Committee of the Mending Apparatus refused to answer it.

"It is too bad!" she exclaimed to another of her friends. "There never was such an unfortunate woman as myself. I can never be sure of my music now. It gets worse and worse each time I summon it."

"I too have my troubles," the friend replied. "Sometimes my ideas are interrupted by a slight jarring noise."

"What is it?"

"I do not know whether it is inside my head, or inside the wall."

"Complain, in either case."

"I have complained, and my complaint will be forwarded in its turn to the Central Committee."

Time passed, and they resented the defects no longer. The defects had not been remedied, but the human tissues in that latter day had become so subservient, that they readily adapted themselves to every caprice of the Machine. The sigh at the crises of the Brisbane symphony no longer irritated Vashti; she accepted it as part of the melody. The jarring noise, whether in the head or in the wall, was no longer resented by her friend. And so with the mouldy artificial fruit, so with the bath water that began to stink, so with the defective rhymes that the poetry machine had taken to emitting. All were bitterly complained of at first, and then acquiesced in and forgotten. Things went from bad to worse unchallenged.

It was otherwise with the failure of the sleeping apparatus. That was a more serious stoppage. There came a day when over the whole world—in Sumatra, in Wessex, in the innumerable cities of Courland and Brazil—the beds, when summoned by their tired owners, failed to appear. It may seem a ludicrous matter, but from it we may date the collapse of humanity. The Committee responsible for the failure was assailed by complainants, whom it referred, as usual, to the Committee of the Mending Apparatus, who in its turn assured them that their complaints would be forwarded to the Central Committee. But the discontent grew, for mankind was not yet sufficiently adaptable to do without sleeping.

"Some one is meddling with the Machine—" they began.

"Someone is trying to make himself king, to reintroduce the personal element."

"Punish that man with Homelessness."

"To the rescue! Avenge the Machine! Avenge the Machine!"

"War! Kill the man!"

But the Committee of the Mending Apparatus now came forward, and allayed the panic with well-chosen words. It confessed that the Mending Apparatus was itself in need of repair.

The effect of this frank confession was admirable.

"Of course," said a famous lecturer—he of the French Revolution, who gilded each new decay with splendour—"of course we shall not press our complaints now. The Mending Apparatus has treated us so well in the past that we all sympathize with it, and will wait patiently for its recovery. In its own good time it will resume its duties. Meanwhile let us do without our beds, our tabloids, our other little wants. Such, I feel sure, would be the wish of the Machine."

Thousands of miles away his audience applauded. The Machine still linked them. Under the seas, beneath the roots of the mountains, ran the wires through which they saw and heard, the enormous eyes and ears that were their heritage, and the hum of many workings clothed their thoughts in one garment of subserviency. Only the old and the sick remained ungrateful, for it was rumoured that Euthanasia, too, was out of order, and that pain had reappeared among men.

It became difficult to read. A blight entered the atmosphere and dulled its luminosity. At times Vashti could scarcely see across her room. The air, too, was foul. Loud were the complaints, impotent the remedies, heroic the tone of the lecturer as he cried: "Courage! courage! What matter so long as the Machine goes on? To it the darkness and the light are one." And though things improved again after a time, the old brilliancy was never recaptured, and humanity never recovered from its entrance into twilight. There was an hysterical talk of "measures," of "provisional dictatorship," and the inhabitants of Sumatra were asked to familiarize themselves with the workings of the central power station, the said power station being situated in France. But for the most part panic reigned, and men spent their strength praying to their Books, tangible proofs of the Machine's omnipotence. There were gradations of terror—at times came rumours of hope—the Mending Apparatus was almost mended—the enemies of the Machine had been got under—new "nerve-centres" were evolving which would do the work even more magnificently than before. But there came a day when, without the slightest warning, without any previous hint of feebleness, the entire communication-system broke down, all over the world, and the world, as they understood it, ended.

Vashti was lecturing at the time and her earlier remarks had been punctuated with applause. As she proceeded the audience became silent, and at the conclusion there was no sound. Somewhat displeased, she called to a friend who was a specialist in sympathy. No sound: doubtless the friend was sleeping. And so with the next friend whom she tried to summon, and so with the next, until she remembered Kuno's cryptic remark, "The Machine stops."

The phrase still conveyed nothing. If Eternity was stopping it would of course be set going shortly.

For example, there was still a little light and air—the atmosphere had improved a few hours previously. There was still the Book, and while there was the Book there was security.

Then she broke down, for with the cessation of activity came an unexpected terror—silence.

She had never known silence, and the coming of it nearly killed her—it did kill many thousands of people outright. Ever since her birth she had been surrounded by the steady hum. It was to the ear what artificial air was to the lungs, and agonizing pains shot across her head. And scarcely knowing what she did, she stumbled forward and pressed the unfamiliar button, the one that opened the door of her cell.

Now the door of the cell worked on a simple hinge of its own. It was not connected with the central power station, dying far away in France. It opened, rousing immoderate hopes in Vashti, for she thought that the Machine had been mended. It opened, and she saw the dim tunnel that curved far away towards freedom. One look, and then she shrank back. For the tunnel was full of people—she was almost the last in that city to have taken alarm.

People at any time repelled her, and these were nightmares from her worst dreams. People were crawling about, people were screaming, whimpering, gasping for breath, touching each other, vanishing in the dark, and ever and anon being pushed off the platform on to the live rail. Some were fighting round the electric bells, trying to summon trains which could not be summoned. Others were yelling for Euthanasia or for respirators, or blaspheming the Machine. Others stood at the doors of their cells fearing, like herself, either to stop in them or to leave them. And behind all the uproar was silence—the silence which is the voice of the earth and of the generations who have gone.

No—it was worse than solitude. She closed the door again and sat down to wait for the end. The disintegration went on, accompanied by horrible cracks and rumbling. The valves that restrained the Medical Apparatus must have weakened, for it ruptured and hung hideously from the ceiling. The floor heaved and fell and flung her from the chair. A tube oozed towards her serpent fashion. And at last the final horror approached—light began to ebb, and she knew that civilization's long day was closing.

She whirled around, praying to be saved from this, at any rate, kissing the Book, pressing button after button.

The uproar outside was increasing, and even penetrated the wall. Slowly the brilliancy of her cell was dimmed, the reflections faded from the metal switches. Now she could not see the reading-stand, now not the Book, though she held it in her hand. Light followed the flight of sound, air was following light, and the original void returned to the cavern from which it has so long been excluded. Vashti continued to whirl, like the devotees of an earlier religion, screaming, praying, striking at the buttons with bleeding hands.

It was thus that she opened her prison and escaped—escaped in the spirit: at least so it seems to me, ere my meditation closes. That she escapes in the body—I cannot perceive that. She struck, by chance, the switch that released the door, and the rush of foul air on her skin, the loud throbbing whispers in her ears, told her that she was facing the tunnel again, and that tremendous platform on which she had seen men fighting. They were not fighting now. Only the whispers remained, and the little whimpering groans. They were dying by hundreds out in the dark.

She burst into tears.

Tears answered her.

They wept for humanity, those two, not for themselves. They could not bear that this should be the end. Ere silence was completed their hearts were opened, and they knew what had been important on the earth. Man, the flower of all flesh, the noblest of all creatures visible, man who had once made god in his image, and had mirrored his strength on the constellations, beautiful naked man was dying, strangled in the garments that he had woven. Century after century had he toiled, and here was his reward. Truly the garment had seemed heavenly at first, shot with colours of culture, sewn with the threads of self-denial. And heavenly it had been so long as man could shed it at will and live by the essence that is his soul, and the essence, equally divine, that is his body. The sin against the body—it was for that they wept in chief; the centuries of wrong against the muscles and the nerves, and those five portals by which we can alone apprehend—glazing it over with talk of evolution, until the body was white pap, the home of ideas as colourless, last sloshy stirrings of a spirit that had grasped the stars.

"Where are you?" she sobbed.

His voice in the darkness said, "Here."

"Is there any hope, Kuno?"

"None for us."

"Where are you?"

She crawled over the bodies of the dead. His blood spurted over her hands.

"Quicker," he gasped, "I am dying—but we touch, we talk, not through the Machine."

He kissed her.

"We have come back to our own. We die, but we have recaptured life, as it was in Wessex, when Ælfrid overthrew the Danes. We know what they know outside, they who dwelt in the cloud that is the colour of a pearl."

"But Kuno, is it true? Are there still men on the surface of the earth? Is this—this tunnel, this poisoned darkness—really not the end?"

He replied:

"I have seen them, spoken to them, loved them. They are hiding in the mist and the ferns until our civilization stops. Today they are the Homeless—tomorrow——"

"Oh, tomorrow—some fool will start the Machine again, tomorrow."

"Never," said Kuno, "never. Humanity has learnt its lesson."

As he spoke, the whole city was broken like a honeycomb. An air-ship had sailed in through the vomitory into a ruined wharf. It crashed downwards, exploding as it went, rending gallery after gallery with its wings of steel. For a moment they saw the nations of the dead, and, before they joined them, scraps of the untainted sky.

1909

THE HORROR OF THE HEIGHTS

Arthur Conan Doyle

The idea that the extraordinary narrative which has been called the Joyce-Armstrong Fragment is an elaborate practical joke evolved by some person, cursed by a perverted and sinister sense of humour, has now been abandoned by all who have examined the matter. The most *macabre* and imaginative of plotters would hesitate before linking his morbid fancies with the unquestioned and tragic facts which reinforce the statement. Though the assertions contained in it are amazing and even monstrous, it is none the less forcing itself upon the general intelligence that they are true, and that we must readjust our ideas to the new situation. This world of ours appears to be separated by a slight and precarious margin of safety from a most singular and unexpected danger. I will endeavour in this narrative, which reproduces the original document in its necessarily somewhat fragmentary form, to lay before the reader the whole of the facts up to date, prefacing my statement by saying that, if there be any who doubt the narrative of Joyce-Armstrong, there can be no question at all as to the facts concerning Lieutenant Myrtle, R. N., and Mr. Hay Connor, who undoubtedly met their end in the manner described.

The Joyce-Armstrong Fragment was found in the field which is called Lower Haycock, lying one mile to the westward of the village of Withyham, upon the Kent and Sussex border. It was on the 15th September last that an agricultural labourer, James Flynn, in the employment of Mathew Dodd, farmer, of the Chauntry Farm, Withyham, perceived a briar pipe lying near the footpath which skirts the hedge in Lower Haycock. A few paces farther on he picked up a pair of broken binocular glasses. Finally, among some nettles in the ditch, he caught sight of a flat, canvas-backed book, which proved to be a note-book with detachable leaves, some of which had come loose and were fluttering along the base of the hedge. These he collected, but some, including the first, were never recovered, and leave a deplorable hiatus in this all-important statement. The note-book was taken by the labourer to his master, who in turn showed it to Dr. J. H. Atherton, of Hartfield. This gentleman at once recognized the need for an expert examination, and the manuscript was forwarded to the Aero Club in London, where it now lies.

The first two pages of the manuscript are missing. There is also one torn away at the end of the narrative, though none of these affect the general coherence of the story. It is conjectured that the missing opening is concerned with the record of Mr. Joyce-Armstrong's qualifications as an aeronaut, which can be gathered from other sources and are admitted to be unsurpassed among the air-pilots of England. For many years he has been looked upon as among the most daring and the most intellectual of flying men, a combination which has enabled him to both invent and test several new devices, including the common gyroscopic attachment which is known by his name. The main body of the manuscript is written neatly in ink, but the last few lines are in pencil and are so ragged as to be hardly legible—exactly, in fact, as they might be expected to appear if they were scribbled off hurriedly from the seat of a moving aeroplane. There are, it may be added, several stains, both on the last page and on the outside cover which have been pronounced by the Home Office experts to be blood—probably human and certainly mammalian. The fact that something closely resembling the organism of malaria was discovered in this blood, and that Joyce-Armstrong is known to have suffered from intermittent fever, is a remarkable example of the new weapons which modern science has placed in the hands of our detectives.

And now a word as to the personality of the author of this epoch making statement. Joyce-Armstrong, according to the few friends who really knew something of the man, was a poet and a dreamer, as well as a mechanic and an inventor. He was a man of considerable wealth, much of which he had spent in the pursuit of his aeronautical hobby. He had four private aeroplanes in his hangars near Devizes, and is said to have made no fewer than one hundred and seventy ascents in the course of last year. He was a retiring man with dark moods, in which he would avoid the society of his fellows. Captain Dangerfield, who knew him better than anyone, says that there were times when his eccentricity threatened to develop into something more serious. His habit of carrying a shot-gun with him in his aeroplane was one manifestation of it.

Another was the morbid effect which the fall of Lieutenant Myrtle had upon his mind. Myrtle, who was attempting the height record, fell from an altitude of something over thirty thousand feet. Horrible to narrate, his head was entirely obliterated, though his body and limbs preserved their configuration. At every gathering of airmen, Joyce-Armstrong, according to Dangerfield, would ask, with an enigmatic smile: "And where, pray, is Myrtle's head?"

On another occasion after dinner, at the mess of the Flying School on Salisbury Plain, he started a debate as to what will be the most permanent danger which airmen will have to encounter. Having listened to successive opinions as to air-pockets, faulty construction, and over-banking, he ended by shrugging his shoulders and refusing to put forward his own views, though he gave the impression that they differed from any advanced by his companions.

It is worth remarking that after his own complete disappearance it was found that his private affairs were arranged with a precision which may show that he had a strong premonition of disaster. With these essential explanations I will now give the narrative exactly as it stands, beginning at page three of the blood-soaked note-book:—

"Nevertheless, when I dined at Rheims with Coselli and Gustav Raymond I found that neither of them was aware of any particular danger in the higher layers of the atmosphere. I did not actually say what was in my thoughts, but I got so near to it that if they had any corresponding idea they could not have failed to express it. But then they are two empty, vainglorious fellows with no thought beyond seeing their silly names in the newspaper. It is interesting to note that neither of them had ever been much beyond the twenty-thousand-foot level. Of course, men have been higher than this both in balloons and in the ascent of mountains. It must be well above that point that the aeroplane enters the danger zone—always presuming that my premonitions are correct.

"Aeroplaning has been with us now for more than twenty years, and one might well ask: Why should this peril be only revealing itself in our day? The answer is obvious. In the old days of weak engines, when a hundred horse-power Gnome or Green was considered ample for every need, the flights were very restricted. Now that three hundred horse-power is the rule rather than the exception, visits to the upper layers have become easier and more common. Some of us can remember how, in our youth, Garros made a world-wide reputation by attaining nineteen thousand feet, and it was considered a remarkable achievement to fly over the Alps. Our standard now has been immeasurably raised, and there are twenty high flights for one in former years. Many of them have been undertaken with impunity. The thirty-thousand-foot level has been reached time after time with no discomfort beyond cold and asthma. What does this prove? A visitor might descend upon this planet a thousand times and never see a tiger. Yet tigers exist, and if he chanced to come down into a jungle he might be devoured. There are jungles of the upper air, and there are worse things than tigers which inhabit them. I believe in time they will map these jungles accurately out. Even at the present moment I could name two of them. One of them lies over the Pau-Biarritz district of France. Another is just over my head as I write here in my house in Wiltshire. I rather think there is a third in the Homburg-Wiesbaden district.

"It was the disappearance of the airmen that first set me thinking. Of course, everyone said that they had fallen into the sea, but that did not satisfy me at all. First, there was Verrier in France; his machine was found near Bayonne, but they never got his body. There was the case of Baxter also, who vanished, though his engine and some of the iron fixings were found in a wood in Leicestershire. In that case, Dr. Middleton, of Amesbury, who was watching the flight with a telescope, declares that just before the clouds obscured the view he saw the machine, which was at an enormous height, suddenly rise perpendicularly upwards in a succession of jerks in a manner that he would have thought to be impossible. That was the last seen of Baxter. There was a correspondence in the papers, but it never led to anything. There were several other similar cases, and then there was the death of Hay Connor. What a cackle there was about an unsolved mystery of the air, and what columns in the halfpenny papers, and yet how little was ever done to get to the bottom of the business! He came down in a tremendous vol-plané from an unknown height. He never got off his machine and died in his pilot's seat. Died of what? 'Heart disease,' said the doctors. Rubbish! Hay Connor's heart was as sound as mine is. What did Venables say? Venables was the only man who was at his side when he died. He said that he was shivering and looked like a man who had been badly scared. 'Died of fright,' said Venables, but could not imagine what he was frightened about. Only said one word to Venables, which sounded like 'Monstrous.' They could make nothing of that at the inquest. But I could make something of it. Monsters! That was the last word of poor Harry Hay Connor. And he *did* die of fright, just as Venables thought.

"And then there was Myrtle's head. Do you really believe—does anybody really believe—that a man's head could be driven clean into his body by the force of a fall? Well, perhaps it may be possible, but I, for one, have never believed that it was so with Myrtle. And the grease upon his clothes—'all slimy with grease,' said somebody at the inquest. Queer that nobody got thinking after that! I did—but, then, I had been thinking for a good long time. I've made three ascents—how Dangerfield used to chaff me about my shot-gun—but I've never been high enough. Now, with this new, light Paul Veroner machine and its one hundred and seventy-five Robur, I should easily touch the thirty thousand tomorrow. I'll have a shot at the record. Maybe I shall have a shot at something else as well. Of course, it's dangerous. If a fellow wants to avoid danger he had best keep out of flying altogether and subside finally into flannel slippers and a dressing-gown. But I'll visit the air-jungle tomorrow—and if there's anything there I shall know it. If I return, I'll find myself a bit of a celebrity. If I don't this note-book may explain what I am trying to do, and how I lost my life in doing it. But no drivel about accidents or mysteries, if *you* please.

"I chose my Paul Veroner monoplane for the job. There's nothing like a monoplane when real work is to be done. Beaumont found that out in very early days. For one thing it doesn't mind damp, and the weather looks as if we should be in the clouds all the time. It's a bonny little model and answers my hand like a tender-mouthed horse. The engine is a ten-cylinder rotary Robur working up to one hundred and seventy-five. It has all the modern improvements—enclosed fuselage, high-curved landing skids, brakes, gyroscopic steadiers, and three speeds, worked by an alteration of the angle of the planes upon the Venetian-blind principle. I took a shot-gun with me and a dozen cartridges filled with buck-shot. You should have seen the face of Perkins, my old mechanic, when I directed him to put them in. I was dressed like an Arctic explorer, with two jerseys under my overalls, thick socks inside my padded boots, a storm-cap with flaps, and my talc goggles. It was stifling outside the hangars, but I was going for the summit of the Himalayas, and had to dress for the part. Perkins knew there was something on and implored me to take him with me. Perhaps I should if I were using the biplane, but a monoplane is a one-man show—if you want to get the last foot of life out of it. Of course, I took an oxygen bag; the man who goes for the altitude record without one will either be frozen or smothered—or both.

"I had a good look at the planes, the rudder-bar, and the elevating lever before I got in. Everything was in order so far as I could see. Then I switched on my engine and found that she was running sweetly. When they let her go she rose almost at once upon the lowest speed. I circled my home field once or twice just to warm her up, and then with a wave to Perkins and the others, I flattened out my planes and put her on her highest. She skimmed like a swallow down wind for eight or ten miles until I turned her nose up a little and she began to climb in a great spiral for the cloud-bank above me. It's all-important to rise slowly and adapt yourself to the pressure as you go.

"It was a close, warm day for an English September, and there was the hush and heaviness of impending rain. Now and then there came sudden puffs of wind from the south-west—one of them so gusty and unexpected that it caught me napping and turned me half-round for an instant. I remember the time when gusts and whirls and air-pockets used to be things of danger—before we learned to put an overmastering power into our engines. Just as I reached the cloud-banks, with the altimeter marking three thousand, down came the rain. My word, how it poured! It drummed upon my wings and lashed against my face, blurring my glasses so that I could hardly see. I got down on to a low speed, for it was painful to travel against it. As I got higher it became hail, and I had to turn tail to it. One of my cylinders was out of action—a dirty plug, I should imagine, but still I was rising steadily with plenty of power. After a bit the trouble passed, whatever it was, and I heard the full, deep-throated purr—the ten singing as one. That's where the beauty of our modern silencers comes in. We can at last control our engines by ear. How they squeal and squeak and sob when they are in trouble! All those cries for help were wasted in the old days, when every sound was swallowed up by the monstrous racket of the machine. If only the early aviators could come back to see the beauty and perfection of the mechanism which have been bought at the cost of their lives!

"About nine-thirty I was nearing the clouds. Down below me, all blurred and shadowed with rain, lay the vast expanse of Salisbury Plain. Half-a-dozen flying machines were doing hackwork at the thousand-foot level, looking like little black swallows against the green background. I dare say they were wondering what I was doing up in cloud-land. Suddenly a grey curtain drew across beneath me and the wet folds of vapours were swirling round my face. It was clammily cold and miserable. But I was above the hail-storm, and that was something gained. The cloud was as dark and thick as a London fog. In my anxiety to get clear, I cocked her nose up until the automatic alarm-bell rang, and I actually began to slide backwards. My sopped and dripping wings had made me heavier than I thought, but presently I was in lighter cloud, and soon had cleared the first layer. There was a second—opal-coloured and fleecy—at a great height above my head, a white, unbroken ceiling above, and a dark, unbroken floor below, with the monoplane labouring upwards upon a vast spiral between them. It is deadly lonely in these cloud-spaces. Once a great flight of some small water-birds went past me, flying very fast to the westwards. The quick whir of their wings and their musical cry were cheery to my ear. I fancy that they were teal, but I am a wretched zoologist. Now that we humans have become birds we must really learn to know our brethren by sight.

"The wind down beneath me whirled and swayed the broad cloud-plain. Once a great eddy formed in it, a whirlpool of vapour, and through it, as down a funnel, I caught sight of the distant world. A large white biplane was passing at a vast depth beneath me. I fancy it was the morning mail service betwixt Bristol and London. Then the drift swirled inwards again and the great solitude was unbroken.

"Just after ten I touched the lower edge of the upper cloud-stratum. It consisted of fine diaphanous vapour drifting swiftly from the westwards. The wind had been steadily rising all this time and it was now blowing a sharp breeze—twenty-eight an hour by my gauge. Already it was very cold, though my altimeter only marked nine thousand. The engines were working beautifully, and we went droning steadily upwards. The cloud-bank was thicker than I had expected, but at last it thinned out into a golden mist before me, and then in an instant I had shot out from it, and there was an unclouded sky and a brilliant sun above my head—all blue and gold above, all shining silver below, one vast, glimmering plain as far as my eyes could reach. It was a quarter past ten o'clock, and the barograph needle pointed to twelve thousand eight hundred. Up I went and up, my ears concentrated upon the deep purring of my motor, my eyes busy always with the watch, the revolution indicator, the petrol lever, and the oil pump. No wonder aviators are said to be a fearless race. With so many things to think of there is no time to trouble about oneself. About this time I noted how unreliable is the compass when above a certain height from earth. At fifteen thousand feet mine was pointing east and a point south. The sun and the wind gave me my true bearings.

"I had hoped to reach an eternal stillness in these high altitudes, but with every thousand feet of ascent the gale grew stronger. My machine groaned and trembled in every joint and rivet as she faced it, and swept away like a sheet of paper when I banked her on the turn, skimming down wind at a greater pace, perhaps, than ever mortal man has moved. Yet I had always to turn again and tack up in the wind's eye, for it was not merely a height record that I was after. By all my calculations it was above little Wiltshire that my air-jungle lay, and all my labour might be lost if I struck the outer layers at some farther point.

"When I reached the nineteen-thousand-foot level, which was about midday, the wind was so severe that I looked with some anxiety to the stays of my wings, expecting momentarily to see them snap or slacken. I even cast loose the parachute behind me, and fastened its hook into the ring of my leathern belt, so as to be ready for the worst. Now was the time when a bit of scamped work by the mechanic is paid for by the life of the aeronaut. But she held together bravely. Every cord and strut was humming and vibrating like so many harp-strings, but it was glorious to see how, for all the beating and the buffeting, she was still the conqueror of Nature and the mistress of the sky. There is surely something divine in man himself that he should rise so superior to the limitations which Creation seemed to impose—rise, too, by such unselfish, heroic devotion as this air-conquest has shown. Talk of human degeneration! When has such a story as this been written in the annals of our race?

"These were the thoughts in my head as I climbed that monstrous, inclined plane with the wind sometimes beating in my face and sometimes whistling behind my ears, while the cloud-land beneath me fell away to such a distance that the folds and hummocks of silver had all smoothed out into one flat, shining plain. But suddenly I had a horrible and unprecedented experience. I have known before what it is to be in what our neighbours have called a *tourbillon*, but never on such a scale as this. That huge, sweeping river of wind of which I have spoken had, as it appears, whirlpools within it which were as monstrous as itself. Without a moment's warning I was dragged suddenly into the heart of one. I spun round for a minute or two with such velocity that I almost lost my senses, and then fell suddenly, left wing foremost, down the vacuum funnel in the centre. I dropped like a stone, and lost nearly a thousand feet. It was only my belt that kept me in my seat, and the shock and breathlessness left me hanging half-insensible over the side of the fuselage. But I am always capable of a supreme effort—it is my one great merit as an aviator. I was conscious that the descent was slower. The whirlpool was a cone rather than a funnel, and I had come to the apex. With a terrific wrench, throwing my weight all to one side, I levelled my planes and brought her head away from the wind. In an instant I had shot out of the eddies and was skimming down the sky. Then, shaken but victorious, I turned her nose up and began once more my steady grind on the upward spiral. I took a large sweep to avoid the danger-spot of the whirlpool, and soon I was safely above it. Just after one o'clock I was twenty-one thousand feet above the sea-level. To my great joy I had topped the gale, and with every hundred feet of ascent the air grew stiller. On the other hand, it was very cold, and I was conscious of that peculiar nausea which goes with rarefaction of the air. For the first time I unscrewed the mouth of my oxygen bag and took an occasional whiff of the glorious gas. I could feel it running like a cordial through my veins, and I was exhilarated almost to the point of drunkenness. I shouted and sang as I soared upwards into the cold, still outer world.

"It is very clear to me that the insensibility which came upon Glaisher, and in a lesser degree upon Coxwell, when, in 1862, they ascended in a balloon to the height of thirty thousand feet, was due to the extreme speed with which a perpendicular ascent is made. Doing it at an easy gradient and accustoming oneself to the lessened barometric pressure by slow degrees, there are no such dreadful symptoms. At the same great height I found that even without my oxygen inhaler I could breathe without undue distress. It was bitterly cold, however, and my thermometer was at zero, Fahrenheit. At one-thirty I was nearly seven miles above the surface of the earth, and still ascending steadily. I found, however, that the rarefied air was giving markedly less support to my planes, and that my angle of ascent had to be considerably lowered in consequence. It was already clear that even with my light weight and strong engine-power there was a point in front of me where I should be held. To make matters worse, one of my sparking-plugs was in trouble again and there was intermittent misfiring in the engine. My heart was heavy with the fear of failure.

"It was about that time that I had a most extraordinary experience. Something whizzed past me in a trail of smoke and exploded with a loud, hissing sound, sending forth a cloud of steam. For the instant I could not imagine what had happened. Then I remembered that the earth is for ever being bombarded by meteor stones, and would be hardly inhabitable were they not in nearly every case turned to vapour in the outer layers of the atmosphere. Here is a new danger for the high-altitude man, for two others passed me when I was nearing the forty-thousand-foot mark. I cannot doubt that at the edge of the earth's envelope the risk would be a very real one.

"My barograph needle marked forty-one thousand three hundred when I became aware that I could go no farther. Physically, the strain was not as yet greater than I could bear but my machine had reached its limit. The attenuated air gave no firm support to the wings, and the least tilt developed into side-slip, while she seemed sluggish on her controls. Possibly, had the engine been at its best, another thousand feet might have been within our capacity, but it was still misfiring, and two out of the ten cylinders appeared to be out of action. If I had not already reached the zone for which I was searching then I should never see it upon this journey. But was it not possible that I had attained it? Soaring in circles like a monstrous hawk upon the forty-thousand-foot level I let the monoplane guide herself, and with my Mannheim glass I made a careful observation of my surroundings. The heavens were perfectly clear; there was no indication of those dangers which I had imagined.

"I have said that I was soaring in circles. It struck me suddenly that I would do well to take a wider sweep and open up a new airtract. If the hunter entered an earth-jungle he would drive through it if he wished to find his game. My reasoning had led me to believe that the air-jungle which I had imagined lay somewhere over Wiltshire. This should be to the south and west of me. I took my bearings from the sun, for the compass was hopeless and no trace of earth was to be seen—nothing but the distant, silver cloud-plain. However, I got my direction as best I might and kept her head straight to the mark. I reckoned that my petrol supply would not last for more than another hour or so, but I could afford to use it to the last drop, since a single magnificent vol-plané could at any time take me to the earth.

"Suddenly I was aware of something new. The air in front of me had lost its crystal clearness. It was full of long, ragged wisps of something which I can only compare to very fine cigarette smoke. It hung about in wreaths and coils, turning and twisting slowly in the sunlight. As the monoplane shot through it, I was aware of a faint taste of oil upon my lips, and there was a greasy scum upon the woodwork of the machine. Some infinitely fine organic matter appeared to be suspended in the atmosphere. There was no life there. It was inchoate and diffuse, extending for many square acres and then fringing off into the void. No, it was not life. But might it not be the remains of life? Above all, might it not be the food of life, of monstrous life, even as the humble grease of the ocean is the food for the mighty whale? The thought was in my mind when my eyes looked upwards and I saw the most wonderful vision that ever man has seen. Can I hope to convey it to you even as I saw it myself last Thursday?

"Conceive a jelly-fish such as sails in our summer seas, bell-shaped and of enormous size—far larger, I should judge, than the dome of St. Paul's. It was of a light pink colour veined with a delicate green, but the whole huge fabric so tenuous that it was but a fairy outline against the dark blue sky. It pulsated with a delicate and regular rhythm. From it there depended two long, drooping, green tentacles, which swayed slowly backwards and forwards. This gorgeous vision passed gently with noiseless dignity over my head, as light and fragile as a soap-bubble, and drifted upon its stately way.

"I had half-turned my monoplane, that I might look after this beautiful creature, when, in a moment, I found myself amidst a perfect fleet of them, of all sizes, but none so large as the first. Some were quite small, but the majority about as big as an average balloon, and with much the same curvature at the top. There was in them a delicacy of texture and colouring which reminded me of the finest Venetian glass. Pale shades of pink and green were the prevailing tints, but all had a lovely iridescence where the sun shimmered through their dainty forms. Some hundreds of them drifted past me, a wonderful fairy squadron of strange argosies of the sky—creatures whose forms and substance were so attuned to these pure heights that one could not conceive anything so delicate within actual sight or sound of earth.

"But soon my attention was drawn to a new phenomenon—the serpents of the outer air. These were long, thin, fantastic coils of vapour-like material, which turned and twisted with great speed, flying round and round at such a pace that the eyes could hardly follow them. Some of these ghost-like creatures were twenty or thirty feet long, but it was difficult to tell their girth, for their outline was so hazy that it seemed to fade away into the air around them. These air-snakes were of a very light grey or smoke colour, with some darker lines within, which gave the impression of a definite organism. One of them whisked past my very face, and I was conscious of a cold, clammy contact, but their composition was so unsubstantial that I could not connect them with any thought of physical danger, any more than the beautiful bell-like creatures which had preceded them. There was no more solidity in their frames than in the floating spume from a broken wave.

"But a more terrible experience was in store for me. Floating downwards from a great height there came a purplish patch of vapour, small as I saw it first, but rapidly enlarging as it approached me, until it appeared to be hundreds of square feet in size. Though fashioned of some transparent, jelly-like substance, it was none the less of much more definite outline and solid consistence than anything which I had seen before. There were more traces, too, of a physical organization, especially two vast, shadowy, circular plates upon either side, which may have been eyes, and a perfectly solid white projection between them which was as curved and cruel as the beak of a vulture.

"The whole aspect of this monster was formidable and threatening, and it kept changing its colour from a very light mauve to a dark, angry purple so thick that it cast a shadow as it drifted between my monoplane and the sun. On the upper curve of its huge body there were three great projections which I can only describe as enormous bubbles, and I was convinced as I looked at them that they were charged with some extremely light gas which served to buoy up the misshapen and semi-solid mass in the rarefied air. The creature moved swiftly along, keeping pace easily with the monoplane, and for twenty miles or more it formed my horrible escort, hovering over me like a bird of prey which is waiting to pounce. Its method of progression—done so swiftly that it was not easy to follow—was to throw out a long, glutinous streamer in front of it, which in turn seemed to draw forward the rest of the writhing body. So elastic and gelatinous was it that never for two successive minutes was it the same shape, and yet each change made it more threatening and loathsome than the last.

"I knew that it meant mischief. Every purple flush of its hideous body told me so. The vague, goggling eyes which were turned always upon me were cold and merciless in their viscid hatred. I dipped the nose of my monoplane downwards to escape it. As I did so, as quick as a flash there shot out a long tentacle from this mass of floating blubber, and it fell as light and sinuous as a whiplash across the front of my machine. There was a loud hiss as it lay for a moment across the hot engine, and it whisked itself into the air again, while the huge, flat body drew itself together as if in sudden pain. I dipped to a vol-piqué, but again a tentacle fell over the monoplane and was shorn off by the propeller as easily as it might have cut through a smoke wreath. A long, gliding, sticky, serpent-like coil came from behind and caught me round the waist, dragging me out of the fuselage. I tore at it, my fingers sinking into the smooth, glue-like surface, and for an instant I disengaged myself, but only to be caught round the boot by another coil, which gave me a jerk that tilted me almost on to my back.

"As I fell over I blazed off both barrels of my gun, though, indeed, it was like attacking an elephant with a pea-shooter to imagine that any human weapon could cripple that mighty bulk. And yet I aimed better than I knew, for, with a loud report, one of the great blisters upon the creature's back exploded with the puncture of the buck-shot. It was very clear that my conjecture was right, and that these vast, clear bladders were distended with some lifting gas, for in an instant the huge, cloud-like body turned sideways, writhing desperately to find its balance, while the white beak snapped and gaped in horrible fury. But already I had shot away on the steepest glide that I dared to attempt, my engine still full on, the flying propeller and the force of gravity shooting me downwards like an aerolite. Far behind me I saw a dull, purplish smudge growing swiftly smaller and merging into the blue sky behind it. I was safe out of the deadly jungle of the outer air.

"Once out of danger I throttled my engine, for nothing tears a machine to pieces quicker than running on full power from a height. It was a glorious, spiral vol-plané from nearly eight miles of altitude—first, to the level of the silver cloud-bank, then to that of the storm-cloud beneath it, and finally, in beating rain, to the surface of the earth. I saw the Bristol Channel beneath me as I broke from the clouds, but, having still some petrol in my tank, I got twenty miles inland before I found myself stranded in a field half a mile from the village of Ashcombe. There I got three tins of petrol from a passing motor-car, and at ten minutes past six that evening I alighted gently in my own home meadow at Devizes, after such a journey as no mortal upon earth has ever yet taken and lived to tell the tale. I have seen the beauty and I have seen the horror of the heights—and greater beauty or greater horror than that is not within the ken of man.

"And now it is my plan to go once again before I give my results to the world. My reason for this is that I must surely have something to show by way of proof before I lay such a tale before my fellow-men. It is true that others will soon follow and will confirm what I have said, and yet I should wish to carry conviction from the first. Those lovely iridescent bubbles of the air should not be hard to capture. They drift slowly upon their way, and the swift monoplane could intercept their leisurely course. It is likely enough that they would dissolve in the heavier layers of the atmosphere, and that some small heap of amorphous jelly might be all that I should bring to earth with me. And yet something there would surely be by which I could substantiate my story. Yes, I will go, even if I run a risk by doing so. These purple horrors would not seem to be numerous. It is probable that I shall not see one. If I do I shall dive at once. At the worst there is always the shotgun and my knowledge of . . ."

Here a page of the manuscript is unfortunately missing. On the next page is written, in large, straggling writing:—

"Forty-three thousand feet. I shall never see earth again. They are beneath me, three of them. God help me; it is a dreadful death to die!"

Such in its entirety is the Joyce-Armstrong Statement. Of the man nothing has since been seen. Pieces of his shattered monoplane have been picked up in the preserves of Mr. Budd-Lushington upon the borders of Kent and Sussex, within a few miles of the spot where the notebook was discovered. If the unfortunate aviator's theory is correct that this air-jungle, as he called it, existed only over the south-west of England, then it would seem that he had fled from it at the full speed of his monoplane, but had been overtaken and devoured by these horrible creatures at some spot in the outer atmosphere above the place where the grim relics were found. The picture of that monoplane skimming down the sky, with the nameless terrors flying as swiftly beneath it and cutting it off always from the earth while they gradually closed in upon their victim, is one upon which a man who valued his sanity would prefer not to dwell. There are many, as I am aware, who still jeer at the facts which I have here set down, but even they must admit that Joyce-Armstrong has disappeared, and I would commend to them his own words: "This note-book may explain what I am trying to do, and how I lost my life in doing it. But no drivel about accidents or mysteries, if *you* please."

1913

THE RED ONE

Jack London

There it was! The abrupt liberation of sound, as he timed it with his watch, Bassett likened it to the trump of an archangel. Walls of cities, he meditated, might well fall down before so vast and compelling a summons. For the thousandth time vainly he tried to analyze the tone-quality of that enormous peal that dominated the land far into the strong-holds of the surrounding tribes. The mountain gorge which was its source rang to the rising tide of it until it brimmed over and flooded earth and sky and air. With the wantonness of a sick man's fancy, he likened it to the mighty cry of some Titan of the Elder World vexed with misery or wrath. Higher and higher it arose, challenging and demanding in such profounds of volume that it seemed intended for ears beyond the narrow confines of the solar system. There was in it, too, the clamor of protest in that there were no ears to hear and comprehend its utterance.

—Such the sick man's fancy. Still he strove to analyze the sound. Sonorous as thunder was it, mellow as a golden bell, thin and sweet as a thrummed taut cord of silver—no; it was none of these, nor a blend of these. There were no words nor semblances in his vocabulary and experience with which to describe the totality of that sound.

Time passed. Minutes merged into quarters of hours, and quarters of hours into half-hours, and still the sound persisted, ever changing from its initial vocal impulse yet never receiving fresh impulse—fading, dimming, dying as enormously as it had sprung into being. It became a confusion of troubled mutterings and babblings and colossal whisperings. Slowly it withdrew, sob by sob, into whatever great bosom had birthed it, until it whimpered deadly whispers of wrath and as equally seductive whispers of delight, striving still to be heard, to convey some cosmic secret, some understanding of infinite import and value. It dwindled to a ghost of sound that had lost its menace and promise, and became a thing that pulsed on in the sick man's consciousness for minutes after it had ceased. When he could hear it no longer, Bassett glanced at his watch. An hour had elapsed ere that archangel's trump had subsided into tonal nothingness.

Was this, then, *his* dark tower?—Bassett pondered, remembering his Browning and gazing at his skeleton-like and fever-wasted hands. And the fancy made him smile—of Childe Roland bearing a slug-horn to his lips with an arm as feeble as his was. Was it months, or years, he asked himself, since he first heard that mysterious call on the beach at Ringmanu? To save himself he could not tell. The long sickness had been most long. In conscious count of time he knew of months, many of them; but he had no way of estimating the long intervals of delirium and stupor. And how fared Captain Bateman of the black-birder *Nari*? he wondered; and had Captain Bateman's drunken mate died of delirium tremens yet?

From which vain speculations, Bassett turned idly to review all that had occurred since that day on the beach of Ringmanu when he first heard the sound and plunged into the jungle after it. Sagawa had protested. He could see him yet, his queer little monkeyish face eloquent with fear, his back burdened with specimen cases, in his hands Bassett's butterfly net and naturalist's shotgun, as he quavered, in Bêche-de-mer English: "Me fella too much fright along bush. Bad fella boy too much stop'm along bush."

Bassett smiled sadly at the recollection. The little New Hanover boy had been frightened, but had proved faithful, following him without hesitancy into the bush in the quest after the source of the wonderful sound. No fire-hollowed tree-trunk, that, throbbing war through the jungle depths, had been Bassett's conclusion. Erroneous had been his next conclusion, namely, that the source or cause could not be more distant than an hour's walk, and that he would easily be back by mid-afternoon to be picked up by the *Nari*'s whale-boat.

"That big fella noise no good, all the same devil-devil," Sagawa had adjudged. And Sagawa had been right. Had he not had his head hacked off within the day? Bassett shuddered. Without doubt Sagawa had been eaten as well by the bad fella boys too much that stopped along the bush. He could see him, as he had last seen him, stripped of the shotgun and all the naturalist's gear of his master, lying on the narrow trail where he had been decapitated barely the moment before. Yes, within a minute the thing had happened. Within a minute, looking back, Bassett had seen him trudging patiently along under his burdens. Then Bassett's own trouble had come upon him. He looked at the cruelly healed stumps of the first and second fingers of his left hand, then rubbed them softly into the indentation in the back of his skull. Quick as had been the flash of the long-handled tomahawk, he had been quick enough to duck away his head and partially to deflect the stroke with his up-flung hand. Two fingers and a hasty scalp-wound had been the price he paid for his life. With one barrel of his ten-gauge shotgun he had blown the life out of the bushman who had so nearly got him; with the other barrel he had peppered the bushmen bending over Sagawa, and had the pleasure of knowing that the major portion of the charge had gone into the one who leaped away with Sagawa's head. Everything had occurred in a flash. Only himself, the slain bushman, and what remained of Sagawa, were in the narrow, wild-pig run of a path. From the dark jungle on either side came no rustle of movement or sound of life. And he had suffered distinct and dreadful shock. For the first time in his life he had killed a human being, and he knew nausea as he contemplated the mess of his handiwork.

Then had begun the chase. He retreated up the pig-run before his hunters, who were between him and the beach. How many there were, he could not guess. There might have been one, or a hundred, for aught he saw of them. That some of them took to the trees and travelled along through the jungle roof he was certain; but at the most he never glimpsed more than an occasional flitting of shadows. No bow-strings twanged that he could hear; but every little while, whence discharged he knew not, tiny arrows whispered past him or struck tree-boles and fluttered to the ground beside him. They were bone-tipped and feather shafted, and the feathers, torn from the breasts of humming-birds, iridesced like jewels.

Once—and now, after the long lapse of time, he chuckled gleefully at the recollection—he had detected a shadow above him that came to instant rest as he turned his gaze upward. He could make out nothing, but, deciding to chance it, had fired at it a heavy charge of number five shot. Squalling like an infuriated cat, the shadow crashed down through tree-ferns and orchids and thudded upon the earth at his feet, and, still squalling its rage and pain, had sunk its human teeth into the ankle of his stout tramping boot. He, on the other hand, was not idle, and with his free foot had done what reduced the squalling to silence. So inured to savagery had Bassett since become, that he chuckled again with the glee of the recollection.

What a night had followed! Small wonder that he had accumulated such a virulence and variety of fevers, he thought, as he recalled that sleepless night of torment, when the throb of his wounds was as nothing compared with the myriad stings of the mosquitoes. There had been no escaping them, and he had not dared to light a fire. They had literally pumped his body full of poison, so that, with the coming of day, eyes swollen almost shut, he had stumbled blindly on, not caring much when his head should be hacked off and his carcass started on the way of Sagawa's to the cooking fire. Twenty-four hours had made a wreck of him—of mind as well as body. He had scarcely retained his wits at all, so maddened was he by the tremendous inoculation of poison he had received. Several times he fired his shotgun with effect into the shadows that dogged him. Stinging day insects and gnats added to his torment, while his bloody wounds attracted hosts of loathsome flies that clung sluggishly to his flesh and had to be brushed off and crushed off.

Once, in that day, he heard again the wonderful sound, seemingly more distant, but rising imperiously above the nearer war-drums in the bush. Right there was where he had made his mistake. Thinking that he had passed beyond it and that, therefore, it was between him and the beach of Ringmanu, he had worked back toward it when in reality he was penetrating deeper and deeper into the mysterious heart of the unexplored island. That night, crawling in among the twisted roots of a banyan tree, he had slept from exhaustion while the mosquitoes had had their will of him.

Followed days and nights that were vague as nightmares in his memory. One clear vision he remembered was of suddenly finding himself in the midst of a bush village and watching the old men and children fleeing into the jungle. All had fled but one. From close at hand and above him, a whimpering as of some animal in pain and terror had startled him. And looking up he had seen her—a girl, or young woman rather, suspended by one arm in the cooking sun. Perhaps for days she had so hung. Her swollen, protruding tongue spoke as much. Still alive, she gazed at him with eyes of terror. Past help, he decided, as he noted the swellings of her legs which advertised that the joints had been crushed and the great bones broken. He resolved to shoot her, and there the vision terminated. He could not remember whether he had or not, any more than could he remember how he chanced to be in that village, or how he succeeded in getting away from it.

Many pictures, unrelated, came and went in Bassett's mind as he reviewed that period of his terrible wanderings. He remembered invading another village of a dozen houses and driving all before him with his shotgun save for one old man, too feeble to flee, who spat at him and whined and snarled as he dug open a ground-oven and from amid the hot stones dragged forth a roasted pig that steamed its essence deliciously through its green-leaf wrappings. It was at this place that a wantonness of savagery had seized upon him. Having feasted, ready to depart with a hind-quarter of the pig in his hand, he deliberately fired the grass thatch of a house with his burning glass.

But seared deepest of all in Bassett's brain, was the dank and noisome jungle. It actually stank with evil, and it was always twilight. Rarely did a shaft of sunlight penetrate its matted roof a hundred feet overhead. And beneath that roof was an aërial ooze of vegetation, a monstrous, parasitic dripping of decadent life-forms that rooted in death and lived on death. And through all this he drifted, ever pursued by the flitting shadows of the anthropophagi, themselves ghosts of evil that dared not face him in battle but that knew that, soon or late, they would feed on him. Bassett remembered that at the time, in lucid moments, he had likened himself to a wounded bull pursued by plains' coyotes too cowardly to battle with him for the meat of him, yet certain of the inevitable end of him when they would be full gorged. As the bull's horns and stamping hoofs kept off the coyotes, so his shotgun kept off these Solomon Islanders, these twilight shades of bushmen of the island of Guadalcanal.

Came the day of the grass lands. Abruptly, as if cloven by the sword of God in the hand of God, the jungle terminated. The edge of it, perpendicular and as black as the infamy of it, was a hundred feet up and down. And, beginning at the edge of it, grew the grass—sweet, soft, tender, pasture grass that would have delighted the eyes and beasts of any husbandman and that extended, on and on, for leagues and leagues of velvet verdure, to the backbone of the great island, the towering mountain range flung up by some ancient earth-cataclysm, serrated and gullied but not yet erased by the erosive tropic rains. But the grass! He had crawled into it a dozen yards, buried his face in it, smelled it, and broken down in a fit of involuntary weeping.

And, while he wept, the wonderful sound had pealed forth—if by *peal*, he had often thought since, an adequate description could be given of the enunciation of so vast a sound so melting sweet. Sweet it was, as no sound ever heard. Vast it was, of so mighty a resonance that it might have proceeded from some brazen-throated monster. And yet it called to him across that leagues-wide savannah, and was like a benediction to his long-suffering, pain racked spirit.

He remembered how he lay there in the grass, wet-cheeked but no longer sobbing, listening to the sound and wondering that he had been able to hear it on the beach of Ringmanu. Some freak of air pressures and air currents, he reflected, had made it possible for the sound to carry so far. Such conditions might not happen again in a thousand days or ten thousand days, but the one day it had happened had been the day he landed from the *Nari* for several hours' collecting. Especially had he been in quest of the famed jungle butterfly, a foot across from wing-tip to wing-tip, as velvet-dusky of lack of colour as was the gloom of the roof, of such lofty arboreal habits that it resorted only to the jungle roof and could be brought down only by a dose of shot. It was for this purpose that Sagawa had carried the twenty-gauge shotgun.

Two days and nights he had spent crawling across that belt of grass land. He had suffered much, but pursuit had ceased at the jungle-edge. And he would have died of thirst had not a heavy thunderstorm revived him on the second day.

And then had come Balatta. In the first shade, where the savannah yielded to the dense mountain jungle, he had collapsed to die. At first she had squealed with delight at sight of his helplessness, and was for beating his brain out with a stout forest branch. Perhaps it was his very utter helplessness that had appealed to her, and perhaps it was her human curiosity that made her refrain. At any rate, she had refrained, for he opened his eyes again under the impending blow, and saw her studying him intently. What especially struck her about him were his blue eyes and white skin. Coolly she had squatted on her hams, spat on his arm, and with her finger-tips scrubbed away the dirt of days and nights of muck and jungle that sullied the pristine whiteness of his skin.

And everything about her had struck him especially, although there was nothing conventional about her at all. He laughed weakly at the recollection, for she had been as innocent of garb as Eve before the fig-leaf adventure. Squat and lean at the same time, asymmetrically limbed, string-muscled as if with lengths of cordage, dirt-caked from infancy save for casual showers, she was as unbeautiful a prototype of woman as he, with a scientist's eye, had ever gazed upon. Her breasts advertised at the one time her maturity and youth; and, if by nothing else, her sex was advertised by the one article of finery with which she was adorned, namely a pig's tail, thrust though a hole in her left ear-lobe. So latcly had the tail been severed, that its raw end still oozed blood that dried upon her shoulder like so much candle-droppings. And her face! A twisted and wizened complex of apish features, perforated by upturned, sky-open, Mongolian nostrils, by a mouth that sagged from a huge upper-lip and faded precipitately into a retreating chin, by peering querulous eyes that blinked as blink the eyes of denizens of monkey-cages.

Not even the water she brought him in a forest-leaf, and the ancient and half-putrid chunk of roast pig, could redeem in the slightest the grotesque hideousness of her. When he had eaten weakly for a space, he closed his eyes in order not to see her, although again and again she poked them open to peer at the blue of them. Then had come the sound. Nearer, much nearer, he knew it to be; and he knew equally well, despite the weary way he had come, that it was still many hours distant. The effect of it on her had been startling. She cringed under it, with averted face, moaning and chattering with fear. But after it had lived its full life of an hour, he closed his eyes and fell asleep with Balatta brushing the flies from him.

When he awoke it was night, and she was gone. But he was aware of renewed strength, and, by then too thoroughly inoculated by the mosquito poison to suffer further inflammation, he closed his eyes and slept an unbroken stretch till sun-up. A little later Balatta had returned, bringing with her a half-dozen women who, unbeautiful as they were, were patently not so unbeautiful as she. She evidenced by her conduct that she considered him her find, her property, and the pride she took in showing him off would have been ludicrous had his situation not been so desperate.

Later, after what had been to him a terrible journey of miles, when he collapsed in front of the devil-devil house in the shadow of the breadfruit tree, she had shown very lively ideas on the matter of retaining possession of him. Ngurn, whom Bassett was to know afterward as the devil-devil doctor, priest, or medicine man of the village, had wanted his head. Others of the grinning and chattering monkey-men, all as stark of clothes and bestial of appearance as Balatta, had wanted his body for the roasting oven. At that time he had not understood their language, if by *language* might be dignified the uncouth sounds they made to represent ideas. But Bassett had thoroughly understood the matter of debate, especially when the men pressed and prodded and felt of the flesh of him as if he were so much commodity in a butcher's stall.

Balatta had been losing the debate rapidly, when the accident happened. One of the men, curiously examining Bassett's shotgun, managed to cock and pull a trigger. The recoil of the butt into the pit of the man's stomach had not been the most sanguinary result, for the charge of shot, at a distance of a yard, had blown the head of one of the debaters into nothingness.

Even Balatta joined the others in flight, and, ere they returned, his senses already reeling from the oncoming fever-attack, Bassett had regained possession of the gun. Whereupon, although his teeth chattered with the ague and his swimming eyes could scarcely see, he held on to his fading consciousness until he could intimidate the bushmen with the simple magics of compass, watch, burning glass, and matches. At the last, with due emphasis, of solemnity and awfulness, he had killed a young pig with his shotgun and promptly fainted.

Bassett flexed his arm-muscles in quest of what possible strength might reside in such weakness, and dragged himself slowly and totteringly to his feet. He was shockingly emaciated; yet, during the various convalescences of the many months of his long sickness, he had never regained quite the same degree of strength as this time. What he feared was another relapse such as he had already frequently experienced. Without drugs, without even quinine, he had managed so far to live through a combination of the most pernicious and most malignant of malarial and black-water fevers. But could he continue to endure? Such was his everlasting query. For, like the genuine scientist he was, he would not be content to die until he had solved the secret of the sound.

Supported by a staff, he staggered the few steps to the devil-devil house where death and Ngurn reigned in gloom. Almost as infamously dark and evil-stinking as the jungle was the devil-devil house—in Bassett's opinion. Yet therein was usually to be found his favorite crony and gossip, Ngurn, always willing for a yarn or a discussion, the while he sat in the ashes of death and in a slow smoke shrewdly revolved curing human heads suspended from the rafters. For, through the months' interval of consciousness of his long sickness, Bassett had mastered the psychological simplicities and lingual difficulties of the language of the tribe of Ngurn and Balatta, and Gngngn—the latter the addle-headed young chief who was ruled by Ngurn, and who, whispered intrigue had it, was the son of Ngurn.

"Will the Red One speak to-day?" Bassett asked, by this time so accustomed to the old man's gruesome occupation as to take even an interest in the progress of the smoke-curing.

With the eye of an expert Ngurn examined the particular head he was at work upon.

"It will be ten days before I can say 'finish,'" he said. "Never has any man fixed heads like these."

Bassett smiled inwardly at the old fellow's reluctance to talk with him of the Red One. It had always been so. Never, by any chance, had Ngurn or any other member of the weird tribe divulged the slightest hint of any physical characteristic of the Red One. Physical the Red One must be, to emit the wonderful sound, and though it was called the Red One, Bassett could not be sure that red represented the color of it. Red enough were the deeds and powers of it, from what abstract clues he had gleaned. Not alone, had Ngurn informed him, was the Red One more bestial powerful than the neighbor tribal gods, ever athirst for the red blood of living human sacrifices, but the neighbor gods themselves were sacrificed and tormented before him. He was the god of a dozen allied villages similar to this one, which was the central and commanding village of the federation. By virtue of the Red One many alien villages had been devastated and even wiped out, the prisoners sacrificed to the Red One. This was true today, and it extended back into old history carried down by word of mouth through the generations. When he, Ngurn, had been a young man, the tribes beyond the grass lands had made a war raid. In the counter raid, Ngurn and his fighting folk had made many prisoners. Of children alone over five score living had been bled white before the Red One, and many, many more men and women.

The Thunderer was another of Ngurn's names for the mysterious deity. Also at times was he called The Loud Shouter, The God-Voiced, The Bird-Throated, The One with the Throat Sweet as the Throat of the Honey-Bird, The Sun Singer, and The Star-Born.

Why the Star-Born? In vain Bassett interrogated Ngurn. According to that old devil-devil doctor, the Red One had always been, just where he was at present, forever singing and thundering his will over men. But Ngurn's father, wrapped in decaying grass-matting and hanging even then over their heads among the smoky rafters of the devil-devil house, had held otherwise. That departed wise one had believed that the Red One came from out of the starry night, else why—so his argument had run—had the old and forgotten ones passed his name down as The Star-Born? Bassett could not but recognize something cogent in such argument. But Ngurn affirmed the long years of his long life, wherein he had gazed upon many starry nights, yet never had he found a star on grass land or in jungle depth—and he had looked for them. True, he had beheld shooting stars (this in reply to Bassett's contention); but likewise had he beheld the phosphorescence of fungoid growths and rotten meat and fireflies on dark nights, and the flames of wood-fires and of blazing candle-nuts; yet what were flame and blaze and glow when they had flamed and blazed and glowed? Answer: memories, memories only, of things which had ceased to be, like memories of matings accomplished, of feasts forgotten, of desires that were the ghosts of desires, flaring, flaming, burning, yet unrealized in achievement of easement and satisfaction. Where was the appetite of yesterday? the roasted flesh of the wild pig the hunter's arrow failed to slay? the maid, unwed and dead ere the young man knew her?

A memory was not a star, was Ngurn's contention. How could a memory be a star? Further, after all his long life he still observed the starry night-sky unaltered. Never had he noted the absence of a single star from its accustomed place. Besides, stars were fire, and the Red One was not fire—which last involuntary betrayal told Bassett nothing.

"Will the Red One speak to-morrow?" he queried.

Ngurn shrugged his shoulders as who should say.

"And the day after?—and the day after that?" Bassett persisted.

"I would like to have the curing of your head," Ngurn changed the subject. "It is different from any other head. No devil-devil has a head like it. Besides, I would cure it well. I would take months and months. The moons would come and the moons would go, and the smoke would be very slow, and I should myself gather the materials for the curing smoke. The skin would not wrinkle. It would be as smooth as your skin now."

He stood up, and from the dim rafters, grimed with the smoking of countless heads, where day was no more than a gloom, took down a matting-wrapped parcel and began to open it.

"It is a head like yours," he said, "but it is poorly cured."

Bassett had pricked up his ears at the suggestion that it was a white man's head; for he had long since come to accept that these jungle-dwellers, in the midmost centre of the great island, had never had intercourse with white men. Certainly he had found them without the almost universal Bêche-de-mer English of the west South Pacific. Nor had they knowledge of tobacco, nor of gunpowder. Their few precious knives, made from lengths of hoop-iron, and their few and more precious tomahawks from cheap trade hatchets, he had surmised they had captured in war from the bushmen of the jungle beyond the grass lands, and that they, in turn, had similarly gained them from the salt-water men who fringed the coral beaches of the shore and had contact with the occasional white men.

"The folk in the out beyond do not know how to cure heads," old Ngurn explained, as he drew forth from the filthy matting and placed in Bassett's hands an indubitable white man's head.

Ancient it was beyond question; white it was as the blond hair attested. He could have sworn it once belonged to an Englishman, and to an Englishman of long before by token of the heavy gold circlets still threaded in the withered ear-lobes.

"Now your head . . ." the devil-devil doctor began on his favorite topic.

"I'll tell you what," Bassett interrupted, struck by a new idea. "When I die I'll let you have my head to cure, if, first, you take me to look upon the Red One."

"I will have your head anyway when you are dead," Ngurn rejected the proposition. He added, with the brutal frankness of the savage: "Besides, you have not long to live. You are almost a dead man now. You will grow less strong. In not many months I shall have you here turning and turning in the smoke. It is pleasant, through the long afternoons, to turn the head of one you have known as well as I know you. And I shall talk to you and tell you the many secrets you want to know. Which will not matter, for you will be dead."

"Ngurn," Bassett threatened in sudden anger. "You know the Baby Thunder in the Iron that is mine." (This was in reference to his all-potent and all-awful shotgun.) "I can kill you any time, and then you will not get my head."

"Just the same, will Gngngn, or some one else of my folk get it," Ngurn complacently assured him. "And just the same will it turn and turn here in the devil-devil house in the smoke. The quicker you slay me with your Baby Thunder, the quicker will your head turn in the smoke."

And Bassett knew he was beaten in the discussion.

What was the Red One?—Bassett asked himself a thousand times in the succeeding week, while he seemed to grow stronger. What was the source of the wonderful sound? What was this Sun Singer, this Star-Born One, this mysterious deity, as bestial-conducted as the black and kinky-headed and monkey-like human beasts who worshipped it, and whose silver-sweet, bull-mouthed singing and commanding he had heard at the taboo distance for so long?

Ngurn had he failed to bribe with the inevitable curing of his head when he was dead. Gngngn, imbecile and chief that he was, was too imbecilic, too much under the sway of Ngurn, to be considered. Remained Balatta, who, from the time she found him and poked his blue eyes open to recrudescence of her grotesque, female hideousness, had continued his adorer. Woman she was, and he had long known that the only way to win from her treason of her tribe was through the woman's heart of her.

Bassett was a fastidious man. He had never recovered from the initial horror caused by Balatta's female awfulness. Back in England, even at best, the charm of woman, to him, had never been robust. Yet now, resolutely, as only a man can do who is capable of martyring himself for the cause of science, he proceeded to violate all the fineness and delicacy of his nature by making love to the unthinkably disgusting bushwoman.

He shuddered, but with averted face hid his grimaces and swallowed his gorge as he put his arm around her dirt-crusted shoulders and felt the contact of her rancid-oily and kinky hair with his neck and chin. But he nearly screamed when she succumbed to that caress so at the very first of the courtship and mowed and gibbered and squealed little, queer, pig-like gurgly noises of delight. It was too much. And the next he did in the singular courtship was to take her down to the stream and give her a vigorous scrubbing.

From then on he devoted himself to her like a true swain as frequently and for as long at a time as his will could override his repugnance. But marriage, which she ardently suggested, with due observance of tribal custom, he balked at. Fortunately, taboo rule was strong in the tribe. Thus, Ngurn could never touch bone, or flesh, or hide of crocodile. This had been ordained at his birth. Gngngn was denied ever the touch of woman. Such pollution, did it chance to occur, could be purged only by the death of the offending female. It had happened once, since Bassett's arrival, when a girl of nine, running in play, stumbled and fell against the sacred chief. And the girl-child was seen no more. In whispers, Balatta told Bassett that she had been three days and nights in dying before the Red One. As for Balatta, the breadfruit was taboo to her. For which Bassett was thankful. The taboo might have been water.

For himself, he fabricated a special taboo. Only could he marry, he explained, when the Southern Cross rode highest in the sky. Knowing his astronomy, he thus gained a reprieve of nearly nine months; and he was confident that within that time he would either be dead or escaped to the coast with full knowledge of the Red One and of the source of the Red One's wonderful voice. At first he had fancied the Red One to be some colossal statue, like Memnon, rendered vocal under certain temperature conditions of sunlight. But when, after a war raid, a batch of prisoners was brought in and the sacrifice made at night, in the midst of rain, when the sun could play no part, the Red One had been more vocal than usual, Bassett discarded that hypothesis.

In company with Balatta, sometimes with men and parties of women, the freedom of the jungle was his for three quadrants of the compass. But the fourth quadrant, which contained the Red One's abiding place, was taboo. He made more thorough love to Balatta—also saw to it that she scrubbed herself more frequently. Eternal female she was, capable of any treason for the sake of love. And, though the sight of her was provocative of nausea and the contact of her provocative of despair, although he could not escape her awfulness in his dream-haunted nightmares of her, he nevertheless was aware of the cosmic verity of sex that animated her and that made her own life of less value than the happiness of her lover with whom she hoped to mate. Juliet or Balatta? Where was the intrinsic difference? The soft and tender product of ultra-civilization, or her bestial prototype of a hundred thousand years before her?—there was no difference.

Bassett was a scientist first, a humanist afterward. In the jungle-heart of Guadalcanal he put the affair to the test, as in the laboratory he would have put to the test any chemical reaction. He increased his feigned ardor for the bushwoman, at the same time increasing the imperiousness of his will of desire over her to be led to look upon the Red One face to face. It was the old story, he recognized, that the woman must pay, and it occurred when the two of them, one day, were catching the unclassified and unnamed little black fish, an inch long, half-eel and half-scaled, rotund with salmon-golden roe, that frequented the fresh water, and that were esteemed, raw and whole, fresh or putrid, a perfect delicacy. Prone in the muck of the decaying jungle-floor, Balatta threw herself, clutching his ankles with her hands kissing his feet and making slubbery noises that chilled his backbone up and down again. She begged him to kill her rather than exact this ultimate love-payment. She told him of the penalty of breaking the taboo of the Red One—a week of torture, living, the details of which she yammered out from her face in the mire until he realized that he was yet a tyro in knowledge of the frightfulness the human was capable of wreaking on the human.

Yet did Bassett insist on having his man's will satisfied, at the woman's risk, that he might solve the mystery of the Red One's singing, though she should die long and horribly and screaming. And Balatta, being mere woman, yielded. She led him into the forbidden quadrant. An abrupt mountain, shouldering in from the north to meet a similar intrusion from the south, tormented the stream in which they had fished into a deep and gloomy gorge. After a mile along the gorge, the way plunged sharply upward until they crossed a saddle of raw limestone which attracted his geologist's eye. Still climbing, although he paused often from sheer physical weakness, they scaled forest-clad heights until they emerged on a naked mesa or tableland. Bassett recognized the stuff of its composition as black volcanic sand, and knew that a pocket magnet could have captured a full load of the sharply angular grains he trod upon.

And then holding Balatta by the hand and leading her onward, he came to it—a tremendous pit, obviously artificial, in the heart of the plateau. Old history, the South Seas Sailing Directions, scores of remembered data and connotations swift and furious, surged through his brain. It was Mendana who had discovered the islands and named them Solomon's, believing that he had found that monarch's fabled mines. They had laughed at the old navigator's child-like credulity; and yet here stood himself, Bassett, on the rim of an excavation for all the world like the diamond pits of South Africa.

But no diamond this that he gazed down upon. Rather was it a pearl, with the depth of iridescence of a pearl; but of a size all pearls of earth and time, welded into one, could not have totaled; and of a color undreamed of in any pearl, or of anything else, for that matter, for it was the color of the Red One. And the Red One himself Bassett knew it to be on the instant. A perfect sphere, fully two hundred feet in diameter, the top of it was a hundred feet below the level of the rim. He likened the color quality of it to lacquer. Indeed, he took it to be some sort of lacquer, applied by man, but a lacquer too marvelously clever to have been manufactured by the bush-folk. Brighter than bright cherry-red, its richness of color was as if it were red builded upon red. It glowed and iridesced in the sunlight as if gleaming up from underlay under underlay of red.

In vain Balatta strove to dissuade him from descending. She threw herself in the dirt; but, when he continued down the trail that spiraled the pit-wall, she followed, cringing and whimpering her terror. That the red sphere had been dug out as a precious thing, was patent. Considering the paucity of members of the federated twelve villages and their primitive tools and methods, Bassett knew that the toil of a myriad generations could scarcely have made that enormous excavation.

He found the pit bottom carpeted with human bones, among which, battered and defaced, lay village gods of wood and stone. Some, covered with obscene totemic figures and designs, were carved from solid tree trunks forty or fifty feet in length. He noted the absence of the shark and turtle gods, so common among the shore villages, and was amazed at the constant recurrence of the helmet motive. What did these jungle savages of the dark heart of Guadalcanal know of helmets? Had Mendana's men-at-arms worn helmets and penetrated here centuries before? And if not, then whence had the bush-folk caught the motive?

Advancing over the litter of gods and bones, Balatta whimpering at his heels, Bassett entered the shadow of the Red One and passed on under its gigantic overhang until he touched it with his finger-tips. No lacquer that. Nor was the surface smooth as it should have been in the case of lacquer. On the contrary, it was corrugated and pitted, with here and there patches that showed signs of heat and fusing. Also, the substance of it was metal, though unlike any metal, or combination of metals, he had ever known. As for the color itself, he decided it to be no application. It was the intrinsic color of the metal itself.

He moved his finger-tips, which up to that had merely rested, along the surface, and felt the whole gigantic sphere quicken and live and respond. It was incredible! So light a touch on so vast a mass! Yet did it quiver under the finger-tip caress in rhythmic vibrations that became whisperings and rustlings and mutterings of sound—but of sound so different; so elusively thin that it was shimmeringly sibilant; so mellow that it was maddening sweet, piping like an elfin horn, which last was just what Bassett decided would be like a peal from some bell of the gods reaching earthward from across space.

He looked at Balatta with swift questioning; but the voice of the Red One he had evoked had flung her face downward and moaning among the bones. He returned to contemplation of the prodigy. Hollow it was, and of no metal known on earth, was his conclusion. It was right-named by the ones of old-time as the Star-Born. Only from the stars could it have come, and no thing of chance was it. It was a creation of artifice and mind. Such perfection of form, such hollowness that it certainly possessed, could not be the result of mere fortuitousness. A child of intelligences, remote and unguessable, working corporally in metals, it indubitably was. He stared at it in amaze, his brain a racing wild-fire of hypotheses to account for this far-journeyer who had adventured the night of space, threaded the stars, and now rose before him and above him, exhumed by patient anthropophagi, pitted and lacquered by its fiery bath in two atmospheres.

But was the color a lacquer of heat upon some familiar metal? Or was it an intrinsic quality of the metal itself? He thrust in the blue-point of his pocket-knife to test the constitution of the stuff. Instantly the entire sphere burst into a mighty whispering, sharp with protest, almost twanging goldenly, if a whisper could possibly be considered to twang, rising higher, sinking deeper, the two extremes of the registry of sound threatening to complete the circle and coalesce into the bull-mouthed thundering he had so often heard beyond the taboo distance.

Forgetful of safety, of his own life itself, entranced by the wonder of the unthinkable and unguessable thing, he raised his knife to strike heavily from a long stroke, but was prevented by Balatta. She upreared on her own knees in an agony of terror, clasping his knees and supplicating him to desist. In the intensity of her desire to impress him, she put her forearm between her teeth and sank them to the bone.

He scarcely observed her act, although he yielded automatically to his gentler instincts and withheld the knife-hack. To him, human life had dwarfed to microscopic proportions before this colossal portent of higher life from within the distances of the sidereal universe. As had she been a dog, he kicked the ugly little bushwoman to her feet and compelled her to start with him on an encirclement of the base. Part way around, he encountered horrors. Even, among the others, did he recognize the sun-shriveled remnant of the nine-years girl who had accidentally broken Chief Gngngn's personality taboo. And, among what was left of these that had passed, he encountered what was left of one who had not yet passed. Truly had the bush-folk named themselves into the name of the Red One, seeing in him their own image which they strove to placate and please with such red offerings.

Farther around, always treading the bones and images of humans and gods that constituted the floor of this ancient charnel-house of sacrifice, he came upon the device by which the Red One was made to send his call singing thunderingly across the jungle-belts and grass lands to the far beach of Ringmanu. Simple and primitive was it as was the Red One's consummate artifice. A great king-post, half a hundred feet in length, seasoned by centuries of superstitious care, carven into dynasties of gods, each superimposed, each helmeted, each seated in the open mouth of a crocodile, was slung by ropes, twisted of climbing vegetable parasites, from the apex of a tripod of three great forest trunks, themselves carved into grinning and grotesque adumbrations of man's modern concepts of art and god. From the striker king-post, were suspended ropes of climbers to which men could apply their strength and direction. Like a battering ram, this king-post could be driven end-onward against the mighty, red-iridescent sphere.

Here was where Ngurn officiated and functioned religiously for himself and the twelve tribes under him. Bassett laughed aloud, almost with madness, at the thought of this wonderful messenger, winged with intelligence across space, to fall into a bushman stronghold and be worshipped by ape-like, man-eating and head-hunting savages. It was as if God's Word had fallen into the muck mire of the abyss underlying the bottom of hell; as if Jehovah's Commandments had been presented on carved stone to the monkeys of the monkey cage at the Zoo; as if the Sermon on the Mount had been preached in a roaring bedlam of lunatics.

The slow weeks passed. The nights, by election, Bassett spent on the ashen floor of the devil-devil house, beneath the ever-swinging, slow-curing heads. His reason for this was that it was taboo to the lesser sex of woman, and therefore, a refuge for him from Balatta, who grew more persecutingly and perilously loverly as the Southern Cross rode higher in the sky and marked the imminence of her nuptials. His days Bassett spent in a hammock swung under the shade of the great breadfruit tree before the devil-devil house. There were breaks in this program, when, in the comas of his devastating fever-attacks, he lay for days and nights in the house of heads. Ever he struggled to combat the fever, to live, to continue to live, to grow strong and stronger against the day when he would be strong enough to dare the grass lands and the belted jungle beyond, and win to the beach, and to some labor-recruiting, black-birding ketch or schooner, and on to civilization and the men of civilization, to whom he could give news of the message from other worlds that lay, darkly worshipped by beastmen, in the black heart of Guadalcanal's midmost center.

On the other nights, lying late under the breadfruit tree, Bassett spent long hours watching the slow setting of the western stars beyond the black wall of jungle where it had been thrust back by the clearing for the village. Possessed of more than a cursory knowledge of astronomy, he took a sick man's pleasure in speculating as to the dwellers on the unseen worlds of those incredibly remote suns, to haunt whose houses of light, life came forth, a shy visitant, from the rayless crypts of matter. He could no more apprehend limits to time than bounds to space. No subversive radium speculations had shaken his steady scientific faith in the conservation of energy and the indestructibility of matter. Always and forever must there have been stars. And surely, in that cosmic ferment, all must be comparatively alike, comparatively of the same substance, or substances, save for the freaks of the ferment. All must obey, or compose, the same laws that ran without infraction through the entire experience of man. Therefore, he argued and agreed, must worlds and life be appanages to all the suns as they were appanages to the particular sun of his own solar system.

Even as he lay here, under the breadfruit tree, an intelligence that stared across the starry gulfs, so must all the universe be exposed to the ceaseless scrutiny of innumerable eyes, like his, though grantedly different, with behind them, by the same token, intelligences that questioned and sought the meaning and the construction of the whole. So reasoning, he felt his soul go forth in kinship with that august company, that multitude whose gaze was forever upon the arras of infinity.

Who were they, what were they, those far distant and superior ones who had bridged the sky with their gigantic, red-iridescent, heaven-singing message? Surely, and long since, had they, too, trod the path on which man had so recently, by the calendar of the cosmos, set his feet. And to be able to send such a message across the pit of space, surely they had reached those heights to which man, in tears and travail and bloody sweat, in darkness and confusion of many counsels, was so slowly struggling. And what were they on their heights? Had they won Brotherhood? Or had they learned that the law of love imposed the penalty of weakness and decay? Was strife, life? Was the rule of all the universe the pitiless rule of natural selection? And, and most immediately and poignantly, were their far conclusions, their long-won wisdoms, shut even then in the huge, metallic heart of the Red One, waiting for the first earth-man to read? Of one thing he was certain: No drop of red dew shaken from the lion-mane of some sun in torment, was the sounding sphere. It was of design, not chance, and it contained the speech and wisdom of the stars.

What engines and elements and mastered forces, what lore and mysteries and destiny-controls, might be there!

Undoubtedly, since so much could be enclosed in so little a thing as the foundation stone of a public building, this enormous sphere should contain vast histories, profounds of research achieved beyond man's wildest guesses, laws and formulae that, easily mastered, would make man's life on earth, individual and collective, spring up from its present mire to inconceivable heights of purity and power. It was Time's greatest gift to blindfold, insatiable, and sky-aspiring man. And to him, Bassett, had been vouchsafed the lordly fortune to be the first to receive this message from man's interstellar kin!

No white man, much less no outland man of the other bush-tribes, had gazed upon the Red One and lived. Such the law expounded by Ngurn to Bassett. There was such a thing as blood brotherhood, Bassett, in return, had often argued in the past. But Ngurn had stated solemnly no. Even the blood brotherhood was outside the favor of the Red One. Only a man born within the tribe could look upon the Red One and live. But now, his guilty secret known only to Balatta, whose fear of immolation before the Red One fast-sealed her lips, the situation was different. What he had to do was to recover from the abominable fevers that weakened him, and gain to civilization. Then would he lead an expedition back, and, although the entire population of Guadalcanal he destroyed, extract from the heart of the Red One the message of the world from other worlds.

But Bassett's relapses grew more frequent, his brief convalescences less and less vigorous, his periods of coma longer, until he came to know, beyond the last promptings of the optimism inherent in so tremendous a constitution as his own, that he would never live to cross the grass lands, perforate the perilous coast jungle, and reach the sea. He faded as the Southern Cross rose higher in the sky, till even Balatta knew that he would be dead ere the nuptial date determined by his taboo. Ngurn made pilgrimage personally and gathered the smoke materials for the curing of Bassett's head, and to him made proud announcement and exhibition of the artistic perfectness of his intention when Bassett should be dead. As for himself, Bassett was not shocked. Too long and too deeply had life ebbed down in him to bite him with fear of its impending extinction. He continued to persist, alternating periods of unconsciousness with periods of semi-consciousness, dreamy and unreal, in which he idly wondered whether he had ever truly beheld the Red One or whether it was a nightmare fancy of delirium.

Came the day when all mists and cob-webs dissolved, when he found his brain clear as a bell, and took just appraisement of his body's weakness. Neither hand nor foot could he lift. So little control of his body did he have, that he was scarcely aware of possessing one. Lightly indeed his flesh sat upon his soul, and his soul, in its briefness of clarity, knew by its very clarity that the black of cessation was near. He knew the end was close; knew that in all truth he had with his eyes beheld the Red One, the messenger between the worlds; knew that he would never live to carry that message to the world—that message, for aught to the contrary, which might already have waited man's hearing in the heart of Guadalcanal for ten thousand years. And Bassett stirred with resolve, calling Ngurn to him, out under the shade of the breadfruit tree, and with the old devil-devil doctor discussing the terms and arrangements of his last life effort, his final adventure in the quick of the flesh.

"I know the law, O Ngurn," he concluded the matter. "Whoso is not of the folk may not look upon the Red One and live. I shall not live anyway. Your young men shall carry me before the face of the Red One, and I shall look upon him, and hear his voice, and thereupon die, under your hand, O Ngurn. Thus will the three things be satisfied: the law, my desire, and your quicker possession of my head for which all your preparations wait."

To which Ngurn consented, adding:

"It is better so. A sick man who cannot get well is foolish to live on for so little a while. Also is it better for the living that he should go. You have been much in the way of late. Not but what it was good for me to talk to such a wise one. But for moons of days we have held little talk. Instead, you have taken up room in the house of heads, making noises like a dying pig, or talking much and loudly in your own language which I do not understand. This has been a confusion to me, for I like to think on the great things of the light and dark as I turn the heads in the smoke. Your much noise has thus been a disturbance to the long-learning and hatching of the final wisdom that will be mine before I die. As for you, upon whom the dark has already brooded, it is well that you die now. And I promise you, in the long days to come when I turn your head in the smoke, no man of the tribe shall come in to disturb us. And I will tell you many secrets, for I am an old man and very wise, and I shall be adding wisdom to wisdom as I turn your head in the smoke."

So a litter was made, and, borne on the shoulders of half a dozen of the men, Bassett departed on the last little adventure that was to cap the total adventure, for him, of living. With a body of which he was scarcely aware, for even the pain had been exhausted out of it, and with a bright clear brain that accommodated him to a quiet ecstasy of sheer lucidness of thought, he lay back on the lurching litter and watched the fading of the passing world, beholding for the last time the breadfruit tree before the devil-devil house, the dim day beneath the matted jungle roof, the gloomy gorge between the shouldering mountains, the saddle of raw limestone, and the mesa of black volcanic sand.

Down the spiral path of the pit they bore him, encircling the sheening, glowing Red One that seemed ever imminent to iridesce from color and light into sweet singing and thunder. And over bones and logs of immolated men and gods they bore him, past the horrors of other immolated ones that yet lived, to the three-king-post tripod and the huge king-post striker.

Here Bassett, helped by Ngurn and Balatta, weakly sat up, swaying weakly from the hips, and with clear, unfaltering, all-seeing eyes gazed upon the Red One.

"Once, O Ngurn," he said, not taking his eyes from the sheening, vibrating surface whereon and wherein all the shades of cherry-red played unceasingly, ever a-quiver to change into sound, to become silken rustlings, silvery whisperings, golden thrummings of cords, velvet pipings of elfland, mellow distances of thunderings.

"I wait," Ngurn prompted after a long pause, the long-handled tomahawk unassumingly ready in his hand.

"Once, O Ngurn," Bassett repeated, "let the Red One speak so that I may see it speak as well as hear it. Then strike, thus, when I raise my hand; for, when I raise my hand, I shall drop my head forward and make place for the stroke at the base of my neck. But, O Ngurn, I, who am about to pass out of the light of day for ever, would like to pass with the wonder-voice of the Red One singing greatly in my ears."

"And I promise you that never will a head be so well cured as yours," Ngurn assured him, at the same time signaling the tribesmen to man the propelling ropes suspended from the king-post striker. "Your head shall be my greatest piece of work in the curing of heads."

Bassett smiled quietly to the old one's conceit, as the great carved log, drawn back through two-score feet of space, was released. The next moment he was lost in ecstasy at the abrupt and thunderous liberation of sound. But such thunder! Mellow it was with preciousness of all sounding metals. Archangels spoke in it; it was magnificently beautiful before all other sounds; it was invested with the intelligence of supermen of planets of other suns; it was the voice of God, seducing and commanding to be heard. And—the everlasting miracle of that interstellar metal! Bassett, with his own eyes, saw color and colors transform into sound till the whole visible surface of the vast sphere was a-crawl and titillant and vaporous with what he could not tell was color or was sound. In that moment the interstices of matter were his, and the interfusings and intermating transfusings of matter and force.

Time passed. At the last Bassett was brought back from his ecstasy by an impatient movement of Ngurn. He had quite forgotten the old devil-devil one. A quick flash of fancy brought a husky chuckle into Bassett's throat. His shotgun lay beside him in the litter. All he had to do, muzzle to head, was to press the trigger and blow his head into nothingness.

But why cheat him? was Bassett's next thought. Head-hunting, cannibal beast of a human that was as much ape as human, nevertheless Old Ngurn had, according to his lights, played squarer than square. Ngurn was in himself a fore-runner of ethics and contract, of consideration, and gentleness in man. No, Bassett decided; it would be a ghastly pity and an act of dishonour to cheat the old fellow at the last. His head was Ngurn's, and Ngurn's head to cure it would be.

And Bassett, raising his hand in signal, bending forward his head as agreed so as to expose cleanly the articulation to his taut spinal cord, forgot Balatta, who was merely a woman, a woman merely and only and undesired. He knew, without seeing, when the razor-edged hatchet rose in the air behind him. And for that instant, ere the end, there fell upon Bassett the shadows of the Unknown, a sense of impending marvel of the rending of walls before the imaginable. Almost, when he knew the blow had started and just ere the edge of steel bit the flesh and nerves it seemed that he gazed upon the serene face of the Medusa, Truth—And, simultaneous with the bite of the steel on the onrush of the dark, in a flashing instant of fancy, he saw the vision of his head turning slowly, always turning, in the devil-devil house beside the breadfruit tree.

1918

THE COMET

W. E. B. Du Bois

He stood a moment on the steps of the bank, watching the human river that swirled down Broadway. Few noticed him. Few ever noticed him save in a way that stung. He was outside the world—"nothing!" as he said bitterly. Bits of the words of the walkers came to him.

"The comet?"

"The comet—"

Everybody was talking of it. Even the president, as he entered, smiled patronizingly at him, and asked:

"Well, Jim, are you scared?"

"No," said the messenger shortly.

"I thought we'd journeyed through the comet's tail once," broke in the junior clerk affably.

"Oh, that was Halley's," said the president; "this is a new comet, quite a stranger, they say—wonderful, wonderful! I saw it last night. Oh, by the way, Jim," turning again to the messenger, "I want you to go down into the lower vaults today."

The messenger followed the president silently. Of course, they wanted *him* to go down to the lower vaults. It was too dangerous for more valuable men. He smiled grimly and listened.

"Everything of value has been moved out since the water began to seep in," said the president; "but we miss two volumes of old records. Suppose you nose around down there,—it isn't very pleasant, I suppose."

"Not very," said the messenger, as he walked out.

"Well, Jim, the tail of the new comet hits us at noon this time," said the vault clerk, as he passed over the keys; but the messenger passed silently down the stairs. Down he went beneath Broadway, where the dim light filtered through the feet of hurrying men; down to the dark basement beneath; down into the blackness and silence beneath that lowest cavern. Here with his dark lantern he groped in the bowels of the earth, under the world.

He drew a long breath as he threw back the last great iron door and stepped into the fetid slime within. Here at last was peace, and he groped moodily forward. A great rat leaped past him and cobwebs crept across his face. He felt carefully around the room, shelf by shelf, on the muddied floor, and in crevice and corner. Nothing. Then he went back to the far end, where somehow the wall felt different. He sounded and pushed and pried. Nothing. He started away. Then something brought him back. He was sounding and working again when suddenly the whole black wall swung as on mighty hinges, and blackness yawned beyond. He peered in; it was evidently a secret vault—some hiding place of the old bank unknown in newer times. He entered hesitatingly. It was a long, narrow room with shelves, and at the far end, an old iron chest. On a high shelf lay the two missing volumes of records, and others. He put them carefully aside and stepped to the chest. It was old, strong, and rusty. He looked at the vast and old-fashioned lock and flashed his light on the hinges. They were deeply incrusted with rust. Looking about, he found a bit of iron and began to pry. The rust had eaten a hundred years, and it had gone deep. Slowly, wearily, the old lid lifted, and with a last, low groan lay bare its treasure—and he saw the dull sheen of gold!

"Boom!"

A low, grinding, reverberating crash struck upon his ear. He started up and looked about. All was black and still. He groped for his light and swung it about him. Then he knew! The great stone door had swung to. He forgot the gold and looked death squarely in the face. Then with a sigh he went methodically to work. The cold sweat stood on his forehead; but he searched, pounded, pushed, and worked until after what seemed endless hours his hand struck a cold bit of metal and the great door swung again harshly on its hinges, and then, striking against something soft and heavy, stopped. He had just room to squeeze through. There lay the body of the vault clerk, cold and stiff. He stared at it, and then felt sick and nauseated. The air seemed unaccountably foul, with a strong, peculiar odor. He stepped forward, clutched at the air, and fell fainting across the corpse.

He awoke with a sense of horror, leaped from the body, and groped up the stairs, calling to the guard. The watchman sat as if asleep, with the gate swinging free. With one glance at him the messenger hurried up to the sub-vault. In vain he called to the guards. His voice echoed and re-echoed weirdly. Up into the great basement he rushed. Here another guard lay prostrate on his face, cold and still. A fear arose in the messenger's heart. He dashed up to the cellar floor, up into the bank. The stillness of death lay everywhere and everywhere bowed, bent, and stretched the silent forms of men. The messenger paused and glanced about. He was not a man easily moved; but the sight was appalling! "Robbery and murder," he whispered slowly to himself as he saw the twisted, oozing mouth of the president where he lay half-buried on his desk. Then a new thought seized him: If they found him here alone—with all this money and all these dead men—what would his life be worth? He glanced about, tiptoed cautiously to a side door, and again looked behind. Quietly he turned the latch and stepped out into Wall Street.

How silent the street was! Not a soul was stirring, and yet it was high-noon—Wall Street? Broadway? He glanced almost wildly up and down, then across the street, and as he looked, a sickening horror froze in his limbs. With a choking cry of utter fright he lunged, leaned giddily against the cold building, and stared helplessly at the sight.

In the great stone doorway a hundred men and women and children lay crushed and twisted and jammed, forced into that great, gaping doorway like refuse in a can—as if in one wild, frantic rush to safety, they had rushed and ground themselves to death. Slowly the messenger crept along the walls, wetting his parched mouth and trying to comprehend, stilling the tremor in his limbs and the rising terror in his heart. He met a business man, silk-hatted and frock-coated, who had crept, too, along that smooth wall and stood now stone dead with wonder written on his lips. The messenger turned his eyes hastily away and sought the curb. A woman leaned wearily against the signpost, her head bowed motionless on her lace and silken bosom. Before her stood a street car, silent, and within—but the messenger but glanced and hurried on. A grimy newsboy sat in the gutter with the "last edition" in his uplifted hand: "Danger!" screamed its black headlines. "Warnings wired around the world. The Comet's tail sweeps past us at noon. Deadly gases expected. Close doors and windows. Seek the cellar." The messenger read and staggered on. Far out from a window above, a girl lay with gasping face and sleevelets on her arms. On a store step sat a little, sweet-faced girl looking upward toward the skies, and in the carriage by her lay—but the messenger looked no longer. The cords gave way—the terror burst in his veins, and with one great, gasping cry he sprang desperately forward and ran,—ran as only the frightened run, shrieking and fighting the air until with one last wail of pain he sank on the grass of Madison Square and lay prone and still.

When he arose, he gave no glance at the still and silent forms on the benches, but, going to a fountain, bathed his face; then hiding himself in a corner away from the drama of death, he quietly gripped himself and thought the thing through: The comet had swept the earth and this was the end. Was everybody dead? He must search and see.

He knew that he must steady himself and keep calm, or he would go insane. First he must go to a restaurant. He walked up Fifth Avenue to a famous hostelry and entered its gorgeous, ghost-haunted halls. He beat back the nausea, and, seizing a tray from dead hands, hurried into the street and ate ravenously, hiding to keep out the sights.

"Yesterday, they would not have served me," he whispered, as he forced the food down.

Then he started up the street,—looking, peering, telephoning, ringing alarms; silent, silent all. Was nobody—nobody—he dared not think the thought and hurried on.

Suddenly he stopped still. He had forgotten. My God! How could he have forgotten? He must rush to the subway—then he almost laughed. No—a car; if he could find a Ford. He saw one. Gently he lifted off its burden, and took his place on the seat. He tested the throttle. There was gas. He glided off, shivering, and drove up the street. Everywhere stood, leaned, lounged, and lay the dead, in grim and awful silence. On he ran past an automobile, wrecked and overturned; past another, filled with a gay party whose smiles yet lingered on their death-struck lips; on past crowds and groups of cars, pausing by dead policemen; at 42nd Street he had to detour to Park Avenue to avoid the dead congestion. He came back on Fifth Avenue at 57th and flew past the Plaza and by the park with its hushed babies and silent throng, until as he was rushing past 72nd Street he heard a sharp cry, and saw a living form leaning wildly out an upper window. He gasped. The human voice sounded in his ears like the voice of God.

"Hello—hello—help, in God's name!" wailed the woman. "There's a dead girl in here and a man and—and see yonder dead men lying in the street and dead horses—for the love of God go and bring the officers——" And the words trailed off into hysterical tears.

He wheeled the car in a sudden circle, running over the still body of a child and leaping on the curb. Then he rushed up the steps and tried the door and rang violently. There was a long pause, but at last the heavy door swung back. They stared a moment in silence. She had not noticed before that he was a Negro. He had not thought of her as white. She was a woman of perhaps twenty-five—rarely beautiful and richly gowned, with darkly-golden hair, and jewels. Yesterday, he thought with bitterness, she would scarcely have looked at him twice. He would have been dirt beneath her silken feet. She stared at him. Of all the sorts of men she had pictured as coming to her rescue she had not dreamed of one like him. Not that he was not human, but he dwelt in a world so far from hers, so infinitely far, that he seldom even entered her thought. Yet as she looked at him curiously he seemed quite commonplace and usual. He was a tall, dark workingman of the better class, with a sensitive face trained to stolidity and a poor man's clothes and hands. His face was soft and slow and his manner at once cold and nervous, like fires long banked, but not out.

So a moment each paused and gauged the other; then the thought of the dead world without rushed in and they started toward each other.

"What has happened?" she cried. "Tell me! Nothing stirs. All is silence! I see the dead strewn before my window as winnowed by the breath of God,—and see——" She dragged him through great, silken hangings to where, beneath the sheen of mahogany and silver, a little French maid lay stretched in quiet, everlasting sleep, and near her a butler lay prone in his livery.

The tears streamed down the woman's cheeks and she clung to his arm until the perfume of her breath swept his face and he felt the tremors racing through her body.

"I had been shut up in my dark room developing pictures of the comet which I took last night; when I came out—I saw the dead!

"What has happened?" she cried again.

He answered slowly:

"Something—comet or devil—swept across the earth this morning and—many are dead!"

"Many? Very many?"

"I have searched and I have seen no other living soul but you."

She gasped and they stared at each other.

"My—father!" she whispered.

"Where is he?"

"He started for the office."

"Where is it?"

"In the Metropolitan Tower."

"Leave a note for him here and come."

Then he stopped.

"No," he said firmly—"first, we must go—to Harlem."

"Harlem!" she cried. Then she understood. She tapped her foot at first impatiently. She looked back and shuddered. Then she came resolutely down the steps.

"There's a swifter car in the garage in the court," she said.

"I don't know how to drive it," he said.

"I do," she answered.

In ten minutes they were flying to Harlem on the wind. The Stutz rose and raced like an airplane. They took the turn at 110th Street on two wheels and slipped with a shriek into 135th.

He was gone but a moment. Then he returned, and his face was gray. She did not look, but said:

"You have lost—somebody?"

"I have lost—everybody," he said, simply—"unless——"

He ran back and was gone several minutes—hours they seemed to her.

"Everybody," he said, and he walked slowly back with something film-like in his hand which he stuffed into his pocket.

"I'm afraid I was selfish," he said. But already the car was moving toward the park among the dark and lined dead of Harlem—the brown, still faces, the knotted hands, the homely garments, and the silence—the wild and haunting silence. Out of the park, and down Fifth Avenue they whirled. In and out among the dead they slipped and quivered, needing no sound of bell or horn, until the great, square Metropolitan Tower hove in sight. Gently he laid the dead elevator boy aside; the car shot upward. The door of the office stood open. On the threshold lay the stenographer, and, staring at her, sat the dead clerk. The inner office was empty, but a note lay on the desk, folded and addressed but unsent:

Dear Daughter:

I've gone for a hundred mile spin in Fred's new Mercedes. Shall not be back before dinner. I'll bring Fred with me.

J.B.H.

"Come," she cried nervously. "We must search the city."

Up and down, over and across, back again—on went that ghostly search. Everywhere was silence and death—death and silence! They hunted from Madison Square to Spuyten Duyvel; they rushed across the Williamsburg Bridge; they swept over Brooklyn; from the Battery and Morningside Heights they scanned the river. Silence, silence everywhere, and no human sign. Haggard and bedraggled they puffed a third time slowly down Broadway, under the broiling sun, and at last stopped. He sniffed the air. An odor—a smell—and with the shifting breeze a sickening stench filled their nostrils and brought its awful warning. The girl settled back helplessly in her seat.

"What can we do?" she cried.

It was his turn now to take the lead, and he did it quickly.

"The long distance telephone—the telegraph and the cable—night rockets and then—flight!"

She looked at him now with strength and confidence. He did not look like men, as she had always pictured men; but he acted like one and she was content. In fifteen minutes they were at the central telephone exchange. As they came to the door he stepped quickly before her and pressed her gently back as he closed it. She heard him moving to and fro, and knew his burdens—the poor, little burdens he bore. When she entered, he was alone in the room. The grim switchboard flashed its metallic face in cryptic, sphinx-like immobility. She seated herself on a stool and donned the bright earpiece. She looked at the mouthpiece. She had never looked at one so closely before. It was wide and black, pimpled with usage; inert; dead; almost sarcastic in its unfeeling curves. It looked—she beat back the thought—but it looked,—it persisted in looking like—she turned her head and found herself alone. One moment she was terrified; then she thanked him silently for his delicacy and turned resolutely, with a quick intaking of breath.

"Hello!" she called in low tones. She was calling to the world. The world *must* answer. Would the world *answer*? Was the world—

Silence!

She had spoken too low.

"Hello!" she cried, full-voiced.

She listened. Silence! Her heart beat quickly. She cried in clear, distinct, loud tones: "Hello—hello—hello!"

What was that whirring? Surely—no—was it the click of a receiver?

She bent close, she moved the pegs in the holes, and called and called, until her voice rose almost to a shriek, and her heart hammered. It was as if she had heard the last flicker of creation, and the evil was silence. Her voice dropped to a sob. She sat stupidly staring into the black and sarcastic mouthpiece, and the thought came again. Hope lay dead within her. Yes, the cable and the rockets remained; but the world—she could not frame the thought or say the word. It was too mighty—too terrible! She turned toward the door with a new fear in her heart. For the first time she seemed to realize that she was alone in the world with a stranger, with something more than a stranger,—with a man alien in blood and culture—unknown, perhaps unknowable. It was awful! She must escape—she must fly; he must not see her again. Who knew what awful thoughts—

She gathered her silken skirts deftly about her young, smooth limbs—listened, and glided into a sidehall. A moment she shrank back: the hall lay filled with dead women; then she leaped to the door and tore at it, with bleeding fingers, until it swung wide. She looked out. He was standing at the top of the alley,—silhouetted, tall and black, motionless. Was he looking at her or away? She did not know—she did not care. She simply leaped and ran—ran until she found herself alone amid the dead and the tall ramparts of towering buildings.

She stopped. She was alone. Alone! Alone on the streets—alone in the city—perhaps alone in the world! There crept in upon her the sense of deception—of creeping hands behind her back—of silent, moving things she could not see,—of voices hushed in fearsome conspiracy. She looked behind and sideways, started at strange sounds and heard still stranger, until every nerve within her stood sharp and quivering, stretched to scream at the barest touch. She whirled and flew back, whimpering like a child, until she found that narrow alley again and the dark, silent figure silhouetted at the top. She stopped and rested; then she walked silently toward him, looked at him timidly; but he said nothing as he handed her into the car. Her voice caught as she whispered:

"Not—that."

And he answered slowly: "No—not that!"

They climbed into the car. She bent forward on the wheel and sobbed, with great, dry, quivering sobs, as they flew toward the cable office on the east side, leaving the world of wealth and prosperity for the world of poverty and work. In the world behind them were death and silence, grave and grim, almost cynical, but always decent; here it was hideous. It clothed itself in every ghastly form of terror, struggle, hate, and suffering. It lay wreathed in crime and squalor, greed and lust. Only in its dread and awful silence was it like to death everywhere.

Yet as the two, flying and alone, looked upon the horror of the world, slowly, gradually, the sense of all-enveloping death deserted them. They seemed to move in a world silent and asleep,—not dead. They moved in quiet reverence, lest somehow they wake these sleeping forms who had, at last, found peace. They moved in some solemn, world-wide *Friedhof*, above which some mighty arm had waved its magic wand. All nature slept until—until, and quick with the same startling thought, they looked into each other's eyes—he, ashen, and she, crimson, with unspoken thought. To both, the vision of a mighty beauty—of vast, unspoken things, swelled in their souls; but they put it away.

Great, dark coils of wire came up from the earth and down from the sun and entered this low lair of witchery. The gathered lightnings of the world centered here, binding with beams of light the ends of the earth. The doors gaped on the gloom within. He paused on the threshold.

"Do you know the code?" she asked.

"I know the call for help—we used it formerly at the bank."

She hardly heard. She heard the lapping of the waters far below,—the dark and restless waters—the cold and luring waters, as they called. He stepped within. Slowly she walked to the wall, where the water called below, and stood and waited. Long she waited, and he did not come. Then with a start she saw him, too, standing beside the black waters. Slowly he removed his coat and stood there silently. She walked quickly to him and laid her hand on his arm. He did not start or look. The waters lapped on in luring, deadly rhythm. He pointed down to the waters, and said quietly:

"The world lies beneath the waters now—may I go?"

She looked into his stricken, tired face, and a great pity surged within her heart. She answered in a voice clear and calm, "No."

Upward they turned toward life again, and he seized the wheel. The world was darkening to twilight, and a great, gray pall was falling mercifully and gently on the sleeping dead. The ghastly glare of reality seemed replaced with the dream of some vast romance. The girl lay silently back, as the motor whizzed along, and looked half-consciously for the elf-queen to wave life into this dead world again. She forgot to wonder at the quickness with which he had learned to drive her car. It seemed natural. And then as they whirled and swung into Madison Square and at the door of the Metropolitan Tower she gave a low cry, and her eyes were great! Perhaps she had seen the elf-queen?

The man led her to the elevator of the tower and deftly they ascended. In her father's office they gathered rugs and chairs, and he wrote a note and laid it on the desk; then they ascended to the roof and he made her comfortable. For a while she rested and sank to dreamy somnolence, watching the worlds above and wondering. Below lay the dark shadows of the city and afar was the shining of the sea. She glanced at him timidly as he set food before her and took a shawl and wound her in it, touching her reverently, yet tenderly. She looked up at him with thankfulness in her eyes, eating what he served. He watched the city. She watched him. He seemed very human,—very near now.

"Have you had to work hard?" she asked softly.

"Always," he said.

"I have always been idle," she said. "I was rich."

"I was poor," he almost echoed.

"The rich and the poor are met together," she began, and he finished:

"The Lord is the Maker of them all."

"Yes," she said slowly; "and how foolish our human distinctions seem—now," looking down to the great dead city stretched below, swimming in unlightened shadows.

"Yes—I was not—human, yesterday," he said.

She looked at him. "And your people were not my people," she said; "but today——" She paused. He was a man,—no more; but he was in some larger sense a gentleman,

—sensitive, kindly, chivalrous, everything save his hands and—his face. Yet yesterday——

"Death, the leveler!" he muttered.

"And the revealer," she whispered gently, rising to her feet with great eyes. He turned away, and after fumbling a moment sent a rocket into the darkening air. It arose, shrieked, and flew up, a slim path of light, and scattering its stars abroad, dropped on the city below. She scarcely noticed it. A vision of the world had risen before her. Slowly the mighty prophecy of her destiny overwhelmed her. Above the dead past hovered the Angel of Annunciation. She was no mere woman. She was neither high nor low, white nor black, rich nor poor. She was primal woman; mighty mother of all men to come and Bride of Life. She looked upon the man beside her and forgot all else but his manhood, his strong, vigorous manhood—his sorrow and sacrifice. She saw him glorified. He was no longer a thing apart, a creature below, a strange outcast of another clime and blood, but her Brother Humanity incarnate, Son of God and great All-Father of the race to be.

He did not glimpse the glory in her eyes, but stood looking outward toward the sea and sending rocket after rocket into the unanswering darkness. Dark-purple clouds lay banked and billowed in the west. Behind them and all around, the heavens glowed in dim, weird radiance that suffused the darkening world and made almost a minor music. Suddenly, as though gathered back in some vast hand, the great cloud-curtain fell away. Low on the horizon lay a long, white star—mystic, wonderful!

And from it fled upward to the pole, like some wan bridal veil, a pale, wide sheet of flame that lighted all the world and dimmed the stars.

In fascinated silence the man gazed at the heavens and dropped his rockets to the floor. Memories of memories stirred to life in the dead recesses of his mind. The shackles seemed to rattle and fall from his soul. Up from the crass and crushing and cringing of his caste leaped the lone majesty of kings long dead. He arose within the shadows, tall, straight, and stern, with power in his eyes and ghostly scepters hovering to his grasp. It was as though some mighty Pharaoh lived again, or curled Assyrian lord. He turned and looked upon the lady, and found her gazing straight at him.

Silently, immovably, they saw each other face to face—eye to eye. Their souls lay naked to the night. It was not lust; it was not love—it was some vaster, mightier thing that needed neither touch of body nor thrill of soul. It was a thought divine, splendid.

Slowly, noiselessly, they moved toward each other—the heavens above, the seas around, the city grim and dead below. He loomed from out the velvet shadows vast and dark. Pearl-white and slender, she shone beneath the stars. She stretched her jeweled hands abroad. He lifted up his mighty arms, and they cried each to the other, almost with one voice, "The world is dead."

"Long live the——"

"Honk! Honk!" Hoarse and sharp the cry of a motor drifted clearly up from the silence below. They started backward with a cry and gazed upon each other with eyes that faltered and fell, with blood that boiled.

"Honk! Honk! Honk! Honk!" came the mad cry again, and almost from their feet a rocket blazed into the air and scattered its stars upon them. She covered her eyes with her hands, and her shoulders heaved. He dropped and bowed, groped blindly on his knees about the floor. A blue flame spluttered lazily after an age, and she heard the scream of an answering rocket as it flew.

Then they stood still as death, looking to opposite ends of the earth.

"Clang—crash—clang!"

The roar and ring of swift elevators shooting upward from below made the great tower tremble. A murmur and babel of voices swept in upon the night. All over the once dead city the lights blinked, flickered, and flamed; and then with a sudden clanging of doors the entrance to the platform was filled with men, and one with white and flying hair rushed to the girl and lifted her to his breast. "My daughter!" he sobbed.

Behind him hurried a younger, comelier man, carefully clad in motor costume, who bent above the girl with passionate solicitude and gazed into her staring eyes until they narrowed and dropped and her face flushed deeper and deeper crimson.

"Julia," he whispered; "my darling, I thought you were gone forever."

She looked up at him with strange, searching eyes.

"Fred," she murmured, almost vaguely, "is the world—gone?"

"Only New York," he answered; "it is terrible—awful! You know,—but you, how did you escape—how have you endured this horror? Are you well? Unharmed?"

"Unharmed!" she said.

"And this man here?" he asked, encircling her drooping form with one arm and turning toward the Negro. Suddenly he stiffened and his hand flew to his hip. "Why!" he snarled. "It's—a—nigger—Julia! Has he—has he dared——"

She lifted her head and looked at her late companion curiously and then dropped her eyes with a sigh.

"He has dared—all, to rescue me," she said quietly, "and I—thank him—much." But she did not look at him again. As the couple turned away, the father drew a roll of bills from his pockets.

"Here, my good fellow," he said, thrusting the money into the man's hands, "take that,—what's your name?"

"Jim Davis," came the answer, hollow voiced.

"Well, Jim, I thank you. I've always liked your people. If you ever want a job, call on me." And they were gone.

The crowd poured up and out of the elevators, talking and whispering.

"Who was it?"

"Are they alive?"

"How many?"

"Two!"

"Who was saved?"

"A white girl and a nigger—there she goes."

"A nigger? Where is he? Let's lynch the damned——"

"Shut up—he's all right—he saved her."

"Saved hell! He had no business——"

"Here he comes."

Into the glare of the electric lights the colored man moved slowly, with the eyes of those that walk and sleep.

"Well, what do you think of that?" cried a bystander; "of all New York, just a white girl and a nigger!"

The colored man heard nothing. He stood silently beneath the glare of the light, gazing at the money in his hand and shrinking as he gazed; slowly he put his other hand into his pocket and brought out a baby's filmy cap, and gazed again. A woman mounted to the platform and looked about, shading her eyes. She was brown, small, and toil-worn, and in one arm lay the corpse of a dark baby. The crowd parted and her eyes fell on the colored man; with a cry she tottered toward him.

"Jim!"

He whirled and, with a sob of joy, caught her in his arms.

1920

THE JAMESON SATELLITE

Neil R. Jones

Prologue: The Rocket Satellite

In the depths of space, some twenty thousand miles from the earth, the body of Professor Jameson within its rocket container cruised upon an endless journey, circling the gigantic sphere. The rocket was a satellite of the huge, revolving world around which it held to its orbit. In the year 1958, Professor Jameson had sought for a plan whereby he might preserve his body indefinitely after his death. He had worked long and hard upon the subject.

Since the time of the Pharaohs, the human race had looked for a means by which the dead might be preserved against the ravages of time. Great had been the art of the Egyptians in the embalming of their deceased, a practice which was later lost to humanity of the ensuing mechanical age, never to be rediscovered. But even the embalming of the Egyptians—so Professor Jameson had argued—would be futile in the face of millions of years, the dissolution of the corpses being just as eventual as immediate cremation following death.

The professor had looked for a means by which the body could be preserved perfectly forever. But eventually he had come to the conclusion that nothing on earth is unchangeable beyond a certain limit of time. Just as long as he sought an earthly means of preservation, he was doomed to disappointment. All earthly elements are composed of atoms which are forever breaking down and building up, but never destroying themselves. A match may be burned, but the atoms are still unchanged, having resolved themselves into smoke, carbon dioxide, ashes, and certain basic elements. It was clear to the professor that he could never accomplish his purpose if he were to employ one system of atomic structure, such as embalming fluid or other concoction, to preserve another system of atomic structure, such as the human body, when all atomic structure is subject to universal change, no matter how slow.

He had then soliloquized upon the possibility of preserving the human body in its state of death until the end of all earthly time—to that day when the earth would return to the sun from which it had sprung. Quite suddenly one day he had conceived the answer to the puzzling problem which obsessed his mind, leaving him awed with its wild, uncanny potentialities.

He would have his body shot into space enclosed in a rocket to become a satellite of the earth as long as the earth continued to exist. He reasoned logically. Any material substance, whether of organic or inorganic origin, cast into the depths of space would exist indefinitely. He had visualized his dead body enclosed in a rocket flying off into the illimitable maw of space. He would remain in perfect preservation, while on earth millions of generations of mankind would live and die, their bodies to molder into the dust of the forgotten past. He would exist in this unchanged manner until that day when mankind, beneath a cooling sun, should fade out forever in the chill, thin atmosphere of a dying world. And still his body would remain intact and as perfect in its rocket container as on that day of the far-gone past when it had left the earth to be hurled out on its career. What a magnificent idea!

At first he had been assailed with doubts. Suppose his funeral rocket landed upon some other planet or, drawn by the pull of the great sun, were thrown into the flaming folds of the incandescent sphere? Then the rocket might continue on out of the solar system, plunging through the endless seas of space for millions of years, to finally enter the solar system of some far-off star, as meteors often enter ours. Suppose his rocket crashed upon a planet, or the star itself, or became a captive satellite of some celestial body?

It had been at this juncture that the idea of his rocket becoming the satellite of the earth had presented itself, and he had immediately incorporated it into his scheme. The professor had figured out the amount of radium necessary to carry the rocket far enough away from the earth so that it would not turn around and crash, and still be not so far away but what the earth's gravitational attraction would keep it from leaving the vicinity of the earth and the solar system. Like the moon, it would forever revolve around the earth.

He had chosen an orbit sixty-five thousand miles from the earth for his rocket to follow. The only fears he had entertained concerned the huge meteors which careened through space at tremendous rates of speed. He had overcome this obstacle, however, and had eliminated the possibilities of a collision with these stellar juggernauts. In the rocket were installed radium repulsion rays which swerved all approaching meteors from the path of the rocket as they entered the vicinity of the space wanderer.

The aged professor had prepared for every contingency, and had set down to rest from his labors, reveling in the stupendous, unparalleled results he would obtain. Never would his body undergo decay; and never would his bones bleach to return to the dust of the earth from which all men originally came and to which they must return. His body would remain millions of years in a perfectly preserved state, untouched by the hoary palm of such time as only geologists and astronomers can conceive.

His efforts would surpass even the wildest dreams of H. Rider Haggard, who depicted the wondrous, embalming practices of the ancient nation of Kor in his immortal novel, "She," wherein Holly, under the escort of the incomparable Ayesha, looked upon the magnificent, lifelike masterpieces of embalming by the long-gone peoples of Kor.

With the able assistance of a nephew, who carried out his instructions and wishes following his death, Professor Jameson was sent upon his pilgrimage into space within the rocket he himself had built. The nephew and heir kept the secret forever locked in his heart.

Generation after generation had passed upon its way. Gradually humanity had come to die out, finally disappearing from the earth altogether. Mankind was later replaced by various other forms of life which dominated the globe for their allotted spaces of time before they too became extinct. The years piled up on one another, running into millions, and still the Jameson Satellite kept its lonely vigil around the earth, gradually closing the distance between satellite and planet, yielding reluctantly to the latter's powerful attraction.

Forty million years later, its orbit ranged some twenty thousand miles from the earth while the dead world edged ever nearer the cooling sun whose dull, red ball covered a large expanse of the sky. Surrounding the flaming sphere, many of the stars could be perceived through the earth's thin, rarefied atmosphere. As the earth cut in slowly and gradually toward the solar luminary, so was the moon revolving ever nearer the earth, appearing like a great gem glowing in the twilight sky.

The rocket containing the remains of Professor Jameson continued its endless travel around the great ball of the earth whose rotation had now ceased entirely—one side forever facing the dying sun. There it pursued its lonely way, a cosmic coffin, accompanied by its funeral cortege of scintillating stars amid the deep silence of the eternal space which enshrouded it. Solitary it remained, except for the occasional passing of a meteor flitting by at a remarkable speed on its aimless journey through the vacuum between the far-flung worlds.

Would the satellite follow its orbit to the world's end, or would its supply of radium soon exhaust itself after so many eons of time, converting the rocket into the prey of the first large meteor which chanced that way? Would it some day return to the earth as its nearer approach portended, and increase its acceleration in a long arc to crash upon the surface of the dead planet? And when the rocket terminated its career, would the body of Professor Jameson be found perfectly preserved or merely a crumbled mound of dust?

Chapter I: 40,000,000 Years After

Entering within the boundaries of the solar system, a long, dark, pointed craft sped across the realms of space towards the tiny point of light which marked the dull red ball of the dying sun which would some day lie cold and dark forever. Like a huge meteor it flashed into the solar system from another chain of planets far out in the illimitable Universe of stars and worlds, heading towards the great red sun at an inconceivable speed.

Within the interior of the space traveler, queer creatures of metal labored at the controls of the space flyer which juggernauted on its way towards the far-off solar luminary. Rapidly it crossed the orbits of Neptune and Uranus and headed sunward. The bodies of these queer creatures were square blocks of a metal closely resembling steel, while for appendages, the metal cube was upheld by four jointed legs capable of movement. A set of six tentacles, all metal, like the rest of the body, curved outward from the upper half of the cubic body. Surmounting it was a queer-shaped head rising to a peak in the center and equipped with a circle of eyes all the way around the head. The creatures, with their mechanical eyes equipped with metal shutters, could see in all directions. A single eye pointed directly upward, being situated in the space of the peaked head, resting in a slight depression of the cranium.

These were the Zoromes of the planet Zor which rotated on its way around a star millions of light years distant from our solar system. The Zoromes, several hundred thousand years before, had reached a stage in science, where they searched for immortality and eternal relief from bodily ills and various deficiencies of flesh and blood anatomy. They had sought freedom from death, and had found it, but at the same time they had destroyed the propensities for birth. And for several hundred thousand years there had been no births and few deaths in the history of the Zoromes.

This strange race of people had built their own mechanical bodies, and by operation upon one another had removed their brains to the metal heads from which they directed the functions and movements of their inorganic anatomies. There had been no deaths due to worn out bodies. When one part of the mechanical men wore out, it was replaced by a new part, and so the Zoromes continued living their immortal lives which saw few casualties. It was true that, since the innovation of the machines, there had been a few accidents which had seen the destruction of the metal heads with their brains. These were irreparable. Such cases had been few, however, and the population of Zor had decreased but little. The machine men of Zor had no use for atmosphere, and had it not been for the terrible coldness of space, could have just as well existed in the ether void as upon some planet. Their metal bodies, especially their metal-encased brains, did require a certain amount of heat even though they were able to exist comfortably in temperatures which would instantly have frozen to death a flesh-and-blood creature.

The most popular pastime among the machine men of Zor was the exploration of the Universe. This afforded them a never-ending source of interest in the discovery of the variegated inhabitants and conditions of the various planets on which they came to rest. Hundreds of space ships were sent out in all directions, many of them being upon their expeditions for hundreds of years before they returned once more to the home planet of far-off Zor.

This particular space craft of the Zoromes had entered the solar system whose planets were gradually circling in closer to the dull red ball of the declining sun. Several of the machine men of the space craft's crew, which numbered some fifty individuals, were examining the various planets of this particular planetary system carefully through telescopes possessing immense power.

These machine men had no names and were indexed according to letters and numbers. They conversed by means of thought impulses, and were neither capable of making a sound vocally nor of hearing one uttered.

"Where shall we go?" queried one of the men at the controls questioning another who stood by his side examining a chart on the wall.

"They all appear to be dead worlds, 4R-3579," replied the one addressed, "but the second planet from the sun appears to have an atmosphere which might sustain a few living creatures, and the third planet may also prove interesting for it has a satellite. We shall examine the inner planets first of all, and explore the outer ones later if we decide it is worth the time."

"Too much trouble for nothing," ventured 9G-721. "This system of planets offers us little but what we have seen many times before in our travels. The sun is so cooled that it cannot sustain the more common life on its planets, the type of life forms we usually find in our travels. We should have visited a planetary system with a brighter sun."

"You speak of common life," remarked 25X-987. "What of the uncommon life? Have we not found life existent on cold, dead planets with no sunlight and atmosphere at all?"

"Yes, we have," admitted 9G-721, "but such occasions are exceedingly rare."

"The possibility exists, however, even in this case," reminded 4R-3579, "and what if we do spend a bit of unprofitable time in this one planetary system—haven't we all an endless lifetime before us? Eternity is ours."

"We shall visit the second planet first of all," directed 25X-987, who was in charge of this particular expedition of the Zoromes, "and on the way there we shall cruise along near the third planet to see what we can of the surface. We may be able to tell whether or not it holds anything of interest to us. If it does, after visiting the second planet, we shall then return to the third. The first world is not worth bothering with."

The space ship from Zor raced on in a direction which would take it several thousand miles above the earth and then on to the planet which we know as Venus. As the space ship rapidly neared the earth, it slackened its speed, so that the Zoromes might examine it closely with their glasses as the ship passed the third planet.

Suddenly, one of the machine men ran excitedly into the room where 25X-987 stood watching the topography of the world beneath him.

"We have found something!" he exclaimed.

"What?"

"Another space ship!"

"Where?"

"But a short distance ahead of us on our course. Come into the foreport of the ship and you can pick it up with the glass."

"Which is the way it's going?" asked 25X-987.

"It is behaving queerly," replied the machine man of Zor. "It appears to be in the act of circling the planet."

"Do you suppose that there really is life on that dead world—intelligent beings like ourselves, and that this is one of their space craft?"

"Perhaps it is another exploration craft like our own from some other world," was the suggestion.

"But not of ours," said 25X-987.

Together, the two Zoromes now hastened into the observation room of the space ship where more of the machine men were excitedly examining the mysterious space craft, their thought impulses flying thick and fast like bodiless bullets.

"It is very small!"

"Its speed is slow!"

"The craft can hold but few men," observed one.

"We do not yet know of what size the creatures are," reminded another. "Perhaps there are thousands of them in that space craft out there. They may be of such a small size that it will be necessary to look twice before finding one of them. Such beings are not unknown."

"We shall soon overtake it and see."

"I wonder if they have seen us?"

"Where do you suppose it came from?"

"From the world beneath us," was the suggestion.

"Perhaps."

Chapter II: The Mysterious Space Craft

The machine men made way for their leader, 25X-987, who regarded the space craft ahead of them critically.

"Have you tried communicating with it yet?" he asked.

"There is no reply to any of our signals," came the answer.

"Come alongside of it then," ordered their commander. "It is small enough to be brought inside our carrying compartment, and we can see with our penetration rays just what manner of creatures it holds. They are intelligent, that is certain, for their space ship does imply as much."

The space flyer of the Zoromes slowed up as it approached the mysterious wanderer of the cosmic void which hovered in the vicinity of the dying world.

"What a queer shape it has," remarked 25X-987. "It is even smaller than I had previously calculated."

A rare occurrence had taken place among the machine men of Zor. They were overcome by a great curiosity which they could not allow to remain unsatiated. Accustomed as they were to witnessing strange sights and still stranger creatures, meeting up with weird adventures in various corners of the Universe, they had now become hardened to the usual run of experiences which they were in the habit of encountering. It took a great deal to arouse their unperturbed attitudes. Something new, however, about this queer space craft had gripped their imaginations, and perhaps a subconscious influence asserted to their minds that here they have come across an adventure radically unusual.

"Come alongside it," repeated 25X-987 to the operator as he returned to the control room and gazed through the side of the space ship in the direction of the smaller cosmic wanderer.

"I'm trying to," replied the machine man, "but it seems to jump away a bit every time I get within a certain distance of it. Our ship seems to jump backward a bit too."

"Are they trying to elude us?"

"I don't know. They should pick up more speed if that is their object."

"Perhaps they are now progressing at their maximum speed and cannot increase their acceleration any more."

"Look!" exclaimed the operator. "Did you just see that? The thing has jumped away from us again!"

"Our ship moved also," said 25X-987. "I saw a flash of light shoot from the side of the other craft as it jumped."

Another machine man now entered and spoke to the commander of the Zorome expedition.

"They are using radium repellent rays to keep us from approaching," he informed.

"Counteract it," instructed 25X-987.

The man left, and now the machine man at the controls of the craft tried again to close with the mysterious wanderer of the space between planets. The effort was successful, and this time there was no glow of repulsion rays from the side of the long metal cylinder.

They now entered the compartment where various objects were transferred from out the depths of space to the interplanetary craft. Then patiently they waited for the rest of the machine men to open the side of their space ship and bring in the queer, elongated cylinder.

"Put it under the penetration ray!" ordered 25X-987. "Then we shall see what it contains!"

The entire group of Zoromes were assembled about the long cylinder, whose low nickel-plated sides shone brilliantly. With interest they regarded the fifteen-foot object which tapered a bit towards its base. The nose was pointed like a bullet. Eight cylindrical protuberances were affixed to the base while the four sides were equipped with fins such as are seen on aerial bombs to guide them in a direct, unswerving line through the atmosphere. At the base of the strange craft there projected a lever, while in one side was a door, which apparently opened outward. One of the machine men reached forward to open it but was halted by the admonition of the commander.

"Do not open it up yet!" he warned. "We are not aware of what it contains!"

Guided by the hand of one of the machine men, a series of lights shone down upon the cylinder. It became enveloped in a haze of light which rendered the metal sides of the mysterious space craft dim and indistinct while the interior of the cylinder was as clearly revealed as if there had been no covering. The machine men, expecting to see at least several, perhaps many, strange creatures moving about within the metal cylinder, stared aghast at the sight they beheld. There was but one creature, and he was lying perfectly still, either in a state of suspended animation or else of death. He was about twice the height of the mechanical men of Zor. For a long time they gazed at him in a silence of thought, and then their leader instructed them.

"Take him out of the container."

The penetration rays were turned off, and two of the machine men stepped eagerly forward and opened the door. One of them peered within at the recumbent body of the weird-looking individual with the four appendages. The creature lay up against a luxuriously upholstered interior, a strap affixed to his chin while four more straps held both the upper and lower appendages securely to the insides of the cylinder. The machine man released these, and with the help of his comrade removed the body of the creature from the cosmic coffin in which they had found it.

"He is dead!" pronounced one of the machine men after a long and careful examination of the corpse. "He has been like this for a long time."

"There are strange thought impressions left upon his mind," remarked another.

One of the machine men, whose metal body was of a different shade than that of his companions, stepped forward, his cubic body bent over that of the strange, cold creature who was garbed in fantastic accoutrements. He examined the dead organism a moment, and then he turned to his companions.

"Would you like to hear his story?" he asked.

"Yes!" came the concerted reply.

"You shall, then," was the ultimatum. "Bring him into my laboratory. I shall remove his brain and stimulate the cells into activity once more. We shall give him life again, transplanting his brain into the head of one of our machines."

With these words he directed two of the Zoromes to carry the corpse into the laboratory.

As the space ship cruised about in the vicinity of this third planet which 25X-987 had decided to visit on finding the metal cylinder with its queer inhabitant, 8B-52, the experimenter, worked unceasingly in his laboratory to revive the long-dead brain cells to action once more. Finally, after consummating his desires and having his efforts crowned with success, he placed the brain within the head of a machine. The brain was brought to consciousness. The creature's body was discarded after the all-important brain had been removed.

Chapter III: Recalled to Life

As Professor Jameson came to, he became aware of a strange feeling. He was sick. The doctors had not expected him to live; they had frankly told him so—but he had cared little in view of the long, happy years stretched out behind him. Perhaps he was not to die yet. He wondered how long he had slept. How strange he felt—as if he had no body. Why couldn't he open his eyes? He tried very hard. A mist swam before him. His eyes had been open all the time but he had not seen before. That was queer, he ruminated. All was silent about his bedside. Had all the doctors and nurses left him to sleep—or to die?

Devil take that mist which now swam before him, obscuring everything in line of vision. He would call his nephew. Vainly he attempted to shout the word "Douglas," but to no avail. Where was his mouth? It seemed as if he had none. Was it all delirium? The strange silence—perhaps he had lost his sense of hearing along with his ability to speak—and he could see nothing distinctly. The mist had transferred itself into a confused jumble of indistinct objects, some of which moved about before him.

He was now conscious of some impulse in his mind which kept questioning him as to how he felt. He was conscious of other strange ideas which seemed to be impressed upon his brain, but this one thought concerning his indisposition clamored insistently over the lesser ideas. It even seemed just as if someone was addressing him, and impulsively he attempted to utter a sound and tell them how queer he felt. It seemed as if speech had been taken from him. He could not talk, no matter how hard he tried. It was no use. Strange to say, however, the impulse within his mind appeared to be satisfied with the effort, and it now put another question to him. Where was he from? What a strange question—when he was at home. He told them as much. Had he always lived there? Why, yes, of course.

The aged professor was now becoming more astute as to his condition. At first it was only a mild, passive wonderment at his helplessness and the strange thoughts which raced through his mind. Now he attempted to arouse himself from the lethargy.

Quite suddenly his sight cleared, and what a surprise! He could see all the way around him without moving his head! And he could look at the ceiling of his room! His room? Was it his room! No—It just couldn't be. Where was he? What were those queer machines before him? They moved on four legs. Six tentacles curled outward from their cubical bodies. One of the machines stood close before him. A tentacle shot out from the object and rubbed his head. How strange it felt upon his brow. Instinctively he obeyed the impulse to shove the contraption of metal from him with his hands.

His arms did not rise, instead six tentacles projected upward to force back the machine. Professor Jameson gasped mentally in surprise as he gazed at the result of his urge to push the strange, unearthly looking machine-caricature from him. With trepidation he looked down at his own body to see where the tentacles had come from, and his surprise turned to sheer fright and amazement. His body was like the moving machine which stood before him! Where was he? What ever had happened to him so suddenly? Only a few moments ago he had been in his bed, with the doctors and his nephew bending over him, expecting him to die. The last words he had remembered hearing was the cryptic announcement of one of the doctors.

"He is going now."

But he hadn't died after all, apparently. A horrible thought struck him! Was this the life after death? Or was it an illusion of the mind? He became aware that the machine in front of him was attempting to communicate something to him. How could it, thought the professor, when he had no mouth. The desire to communicate an idea to him became more insistent. The suggestion of the machine man's question was in his mind. Telepathy, thought he.

The creature was asking about the place whence he had come. He didn't know; his mind was in such a turmoil of thoughts and conflicting ideas. He allowed himself to be led to a window where the machine with waving tentacle pointed towards an object outside. It was a queer sensation to be walking on the four metal legs. He looked from the window and he saw that which caused him to nearly drop over, so astounded was he.

The professor found himself gazing out from the boundless depths of space across the cosmic void to where a huge planet lay quiet. Now he was sure it was an illusion which made his mind and sight behave so queerly. He was troubled by a very strange dream. Carefully he examined the topography of the gigantic globe which rested off in the distance. At the same time he could see back of him the concourse of mechanical creatures crowding up behind him, and he was aware of a telepathic conversation which was being carried on behind him—or just before him. Which was it now? Eyes extended all the way around his head, while there existed no difference on any of the four sides of his cubed body. His mechanical legs were capable of moving in any of four given directions with perfect ease, he discovered.

The planet was not the earth—of that he was sure. None of the familiar continents lay before his eyes. And then he saw the great dull red ball of the dying sun. That was not the sun of his earth. It had been a great deal more brilliant.

"Did you come from that planet?" came the thought impulse from the mechanism by his side.

"No," he returned.

He then allowed the machine men—for he assumed that they were machine men, and he reasoned that, somehow or other they had by some marvelous transformation made him over just as they were—to lead him through the craft of which he now took notice for the first time. It was an interplanetary flyer, or space ship, he firmly believed.

25X-987 now took him to the compartment which they had removed him to from the strange container they had found wandering in the vicinity of the nearby world. There they showed him the long cylinder.

"It's my rocket satellite!" exclaimed Professor Jameson to himself, though in reality every one of the machine men received his thoughts plainly. "What is it doing here?"

"We found your dead body within it," answered 25X-987. "Your brain was removed to the machine after having been stimulated into activity once more. Your carcass was thrown away."

Professor Jameson just stood dumfounded by the words of the machine man.

"So I did die!" exclaimed the professor. "And my body was placed within the rocket to remain in everlasting preservation until the end of all earthly time! Success! I have now attained unrivaled success!"

He then turned to the machine man.

"How long have I been that way?" he asked excitedly.

"How should we know?" replied the Zorome. "We picked up your rocket only a short time ago, which, according to your computation, would be less than a day. This is our first visit to your planetary system and we chanced upon your rocket. So it is a satellite? We didn't watch it long enough to discover whether or not it was a satellite. At first we thought it to be another traveling space craft, but when it refused to answer our signals we investigated."

"And so that was the earth at which I looked," mused the professor. "No wonder I didn't recognize it. The topography has changed so much. How different the sun appears—it must have been over a million years ago when I died!"

"Many millions," corrected 25X-987. "Suns of such size as this one do not cool in so short a time as you suggest."

Professor Jameson, in spite of all his amazing computations before his death, was staggered by the reality.

"Who are you?" he suddenly asked.

"We are the Zoromes from Zor, a planet of a sun far across the Universe."

25X-987 then went on to tell Professor Jameson something about how the Zoromes had attained their high stage of development and had instantly put a stop to all birth, evolution and death of their people, by becoming machine men.

Chapter IV: The Dying World

"And now tell us of yourself," said 25X-987, "and about your world."

Professor Jameson, noted in college as a lecturer of no mean ability and perfectly capable of relating intelligently to them the story of the earth's history, evolution and march of events following the birth of civilization up until the time when he died, began his story. The mental speech hampered him for a time, but he soon became accustomed to it so as to use it easily, and he found it preferable to vocal speech after a while. The Zoromes listened interestedly to the long account until Professor Jameson had finished.

"My nephew," concluded the professor, "evidently obeyed my instructions and placed my body in the rocket I had built, shooting it out into space where I became the satellite of the earth for these many millions of years."

"Do you really want to know how long you were dead before we found you?" asked 25X-987. "It would be interesting to find out."

"Yes, I should like very much to know," replied the professor.

"Our greatest mathematician, 459C-79, will tell it to you." The mathematician stepped forward. Upon one side of his cube were many buttons arranged in long columns and squares.

"What is your unit of measuring?" he asked.

"A mile."

"How many times more is a mile than is the length of your rocket satellite?"

"My rocket is fifteen feet long. A mile is five thousand two hundred and eighty feet."

The mathematician depressed a few buttons.

"How far, or how many miles from the sun was your planet at that time?"

"Ninety-three million miles," was the reply.

"And your world's satellite—which you call moon from your planet—earth?"

"Two hundred and forty thousand miles."

"And your rocket?"

"I figured it to go about sixty-five thousand miles from the earth."

"It was only twenty thousand miles from the earth when we picked it up," said the mathematician, depressing a few more buttons. "The moon and sun are also much nearer your planet now."

Professor Jameson gave way to a mental ejaculation of amazement.

"Do you know how long you have cruised around the planet in your own satellite?" said the mathematician. "Since you began that journey, the planet which you call the earth has revolved around the sun over forty million times."

"Forty—million—years!" exclaimed Professor Jameson haltingly. "Humanity must then have all perished from the earth long ago! I'm the last man on earth!"

"It is a dead world now," interjected 25X-987.

"Of course," elucidated the mathematician, "those last few million years are much shorter than the ones in which you lived. The earth's orbit is of less diameter and its speed of revolution is greatly increased, due to its proximity to the cooling sun. I should say that your year was some four times as long as the time in which it now takes your old planet to circumnavigate the sun."

"How many days were there in your year?"

"Three hundred and sixty-five."

"The planet has now ceased rotating entirely."

"Seems queer that your rocket satellite should avoid the meteors so long," observed 459C-79, the mathematician.

"Automatic radium repulsion rays," explained the professor.

"The very rays which kept us from approaching your rocket," stated 25X-987, "until we neutralized them."

"You died and were shot out into space long before any life occurred on Zor," soliloquized one of the machine men. "Our people had not yet even been born when yours had probably disappeared entirely from the face of the earth."

"Hearken to 72N-4783," said 25X-987, "he is our philosopher, and he just loves to dwell on the past life of Zor when we were flesh and blood creatures with the threat of death hanging always over our heads. At that time, like the life you knew, we were born, we lived and died, all within a very short time, comparatively."

"Of course, time has come to mean nothing to us, especially when we are out in space," observed 72N-4783. "We never keep track of it on our expeditions, though back in Zor such accounts are accurately kept. By the way, do you know how long we stood here while you recounted to us the history of your planet? Our machine bodies never get tired, you know."

"Well," ruminated Professor Jameson, giving a generous allowance of time. "I should say about a half a day, although it seemed scarcely as long as that."

"We listened to you for four days," replied 72N-4783.

Professor Jameson was really aghast.

"Really, I hadn't meant to be such a bore," he apologized.

"That is nothing," replied the other. "Your story was interesting, and if it had been twice as long, it would not have mattered, nor would it have seemed any longer. Time is merely relative, and in space actual time does not exist at all, any more than your forty million years' cessation of life seemed more than a few moments to you. We saw that it was so when your first thought impressions reached us following your revival."

"Let us continue on to your planet earth," then said 25X-987. "Perhaps we shall find more startling disclosures there."

As the space ship of the Zoromes approached the sphere from which Professor Jameson had been hurled in his rocket forty million years before, the professor was wondering how the earth would appear, and what radical changes he would find. Already he knew that the geographical conditions of the various continents were changed. He had seen as much from the space ship.

A short time later the earth was reached. The space travelers from Zor, as well as Professor Jameson, emerged from the cosmic flyer to walk upon the surface of the planet. The earth had ceased rotating, leaving one-half its surface always toward the sun. This side of the earth was heated to a considerable degree, while its antipodes, turned always away from the solar luminary, was a cold, frigid, desolate waste. The space travelers from Zor did not dare to advance very far into either hemisphere, but landed on the narrow, thousand-mile strip of territory separating the earth's frozen half from its sun-baked antipodes.

As Professor Jameson emerged from the space ship with 25X-987, he stared in awe at the great transformation four hundred thousand centuries had wrought. The earth's surface, its sky and the sun were all so changed and unearthly appearing. Off to the east the blood red ball of the slowly cooling sun rested upon the horizon, lighting up the eternal day. The earth's rotation had ceased entirely, and it hung motionless in the sky as it revolved around its solar parent, its orbit slowly but surely cutting in toward the great body of the sun. The two inner planets, Mercury and Venus, were now very close to the blood red orb whose scintillating, dazzling brilliance had been lost in its cooling process. Soon, the two nearer planets would succumb to the great pull of the solar luminary and return to the flaming folds, from which they had been hurled out as gaseous bodies in the dim, age-old past, when their careers had just begun.

The atmosphere was nearly gone, so rarefied had it become, and through it Professor Jameson could view with amazing clarity without discomfort to his eyes the bloated body of the dying sun. It appeared many times the size he had seen it at the time of his death, on account of its relative nearness. The earth had advanced a great deal closer to the great star around which it swung.

The sky towards the west was pitch black except for the iridescent twinkle of the fiery stars which studded that section of the heavens. As he watched, a faint glow suffused the western sky, gradually growing brighter, the full moon majestically lifted itself above the horizon, casting its pale, ethereal radiance upon the dying world beneath. It was increased to many times the size Professor Jameson had ever seen it during his natural lifetime. The earth's greater attraction was drawing upon the moon just as the sun was pulling the earth ever nearer itself.

This cheerless landscape confronting the professor represented the state of existence to which the earth had come. It was a magnificent spread of loneliness which bore no witness to the fact that it had seen the teeming of life in better ages long ago. The weird, yet beautiful scene, spread in a melancholy panorama before his eyes, drove his thoughts into gloomy abstraction with its dismal, depressing influence. Its funereal, oppressive aspect smote him suddenly with the chill of a terrible loneliness.

25X-987 aroused Professor Jameson from his lethargic reverie. "Let us walk around and see what we can find. I can understand how you feel in regard to the past. It is quite a shock—but it must happen to all worlds sooner or later—even to Zor. When that time comes, the Zoromes will find a new planet on which to live. If you travel with us, you will become accustomed to the sight of seeing dead, lifeless worlds as well as new and beautiful ones pulsating with life and energy. Of course, this world being your own, holds a peculiar sentimental value to you, but it is really one planet among billions."

Professor Jameson was silent.

"I wonder whether or not there are any ruins here to be found?" queried 25X-987.

"I don't believe so," replied the professor. "I remember hearing an eminent scientist of my day state that, given fifty thousand years, every structure and other creation of man would be obliterated entirely from off the earth's surface."

"And he was right," endorsed the machine man of Zor. "Time is a great effacer."

For a long time the machine men wandered over the dreary surface of the earth, and then 25X-987 suggested a change of territory to explore. In the space ship, they moved around the earth to the other side, still keeping to the belt of shadowland which completely encircled the globe like some gigantic ring. Where they now landed arose a series of cones with hollow peaks.

"Volcanoes!" exclaimed the professor.

"Extinct ones," added the machine man.

Leaving the space ship, the fifty or more machine men, including also Professor Jameson, were soon exploring the curiously shaped peaks. The professor, in his wanderings, had strayed away from the rest, and now advanced into one of the cup-like depressions of the peak, out of sight of his companions, the Zoromes.

Chapter V: Eternity or Death

He was well in the center of the cavity when the soft ground beneath him gave way suddenly and he catapulted below into the darkness. Through the Stygian gloom he fell in what seemed to be an endless drop. He finally crashed upon something hard. The thin crust of the volcano's mouth had broken through, precipitating him into the deep, hollow interior.

It must have been a long ways to fall—or so it had seemed. Why was he not knocked senseless or killed? Then he felt himself over with three tentacles. His metal legs were four broken, twisted masses of metal, while the lower half of his cubic body was jammed out of shape and split. He could not move, and half of his six tentacles were paralyzed.

How would he ever get out of there? he wondered. The machine men of Zor might never find him. What would happen to him, then? He would remain in this deathless, monotonous state forever in the black hole of the volcano's interior unable to move. What a horrible thought! He could not starve to death; eating was unknown among the Zoromes, the machines requiring no food. He could not even commit suicide. The only way for him to die would be to smash the strong metal head, and in his present immovable condition, this was impossible.

It suddenly occurred to him to radiate thoughts for help. Would the Zoromes receive his messages? He wondered how far the telepathic messages would carry. He concentrated the powers of his mind upon the call for help, and repeatedly stated his position and plight. He then left his mind clear to receive the thought answers of the Zoromes. He received none. Again he tried. Still he received no welcoming answer. Professor Jameson became dejected.

It was hopeless. The telepathic messages had not reached the machine men of Zor. They were too far away, just as one person may be out of earshot of another's voice. He was doomed to a terrible fate of existence! It were better that his rocket had never been found. He wished that the Zoromes had destroyed him instead of bringing him back to life—back to this!

His thoughts were suddenly broken in upon.

"We're coming!"

"Don't give up hope!"

If the professor's machine body had been equipped with a heart, it would have sung for joy at these welcome thought impressions. A short time later there appeared in the ragged break of the volcano's mouth, where he had fallen through, the metal head of one of the machine men.

"We shall have you out of there soon," he said.

The professor never knew how they managed it for he lost consciousness under some strange ray of light they projected down upon him in his prison. When he came to consciousness once more, it was to find himself inside the space ship.

"If you had fallen and had smashed your head, it would have been all over with you," were the first thought impulses which greeted him. "As it is, however, we can fix you up first rate."

"Why didn't you answer the first time I called to you?" asked the professor. "Didn't you hear me?"

"We heard you, and we answered, but you didn't hear us. You see, your brain is different than ours, and though you can send thought waves as far as we can you cannot receive them from such a great distance."

"I'm wrecked," said the professor, gazing at his twisted limbs, paralyzed tentacles and jammed body.

"We shall repair you," came the reply. "It is your good fortune that your head was not crushed."

"What are you going to do with me?" queried the professor. "Will you remove my brains to another machine?"

"No, it isn't necessary. We shall merely remove your head and place it upon another machine body."

The Zoromes immediately set to work upon the task, and soon had Professor Jameson's metal head removed from the machine which he had wrecked in his fall down the crater. All during the painless operation, the professor kept up a series of thought exchanges in conversation with the Zoromes, and it seemed but a short time before his head surmounted a new machine and he was ready for further exploration. In the course of his operation, the space ship had moved to a new position, and now as they emerged 25X-987 kept company with Professor Jameson.

"I must keep an eye on you," he said. "You will be getting into more trouble before you get accustomed to the metal bodies."

But Professor Jameson was doing a great deal of thinking. Doubtlessly, these strange machine men who had picked up his rocket in the depths of space and had brought him back to life, were expecting him to travel with them and become adopted into the ranks of the Zoromes. Did he want to go with them? He couldn't decide. He had forgotten that the machine men could read his innermost thoughts.

"You wish to remain here alone upon the earth?" asked 25X-987. "It is your privilege if you really want it so."

"I don't know," replied Professor Jameson truthfully.

He gazed at the dust around his feet. It had probably been the composition of men, and had changed from time to time into various other atomic structures—of other queer forms of life which had succeeded mankind. It was the law of the atom which never died. And now he had within his power perpetual existence. He could be immortal if he wished! It would be an immortality of never-ending adventures in the vast, endless Universe among the galaxy of stars and planets.

A great loneliness seized him. Would he be happy among these machine men of another far-off world—among these Zoromes? They were kindly and solicitous of his welfare. What better fate could he expect? Still, a longing for his own kind arose in him—the call of humanity. It was irresistible. What could he do? Was it not in vain? Humanity had long since disappeared from the earth—millions of years ago. He wondered what lay beyond the pales of death—the real death, where the body decomposed and wasted away to return to the dust of the earth and assume new atomic structures.

He had begun to wonder whether or not he had been dead all these forty millions of years—suppose he had been merely in a state of suspended animation. He had remembered a scientist of his day, who had claimed that the body does not die at the point of official death. According to the claims of this man, the cells of the body did not die at the moment at which respiration, heart beats and the blood circulation ceased, but it existed in the semblance of life for several days afterward, especially in the cells of the bones, which died last of all.

Perhaps when he had been sent out into space in his rocket right after his death, the action of the cosmic void was to halt his slow death of the cells in his body, and hold him in suspended animation during the ensuing millions of years. Suppose he should really die—destroying his own brain? What lay beyond real death? Would it be a better plane of existence than the Zoromes could offer him? Would he rediscover humanity, or had they long since arisen to higher planes of existence or reincarnation? Did time exist beyond the mysterious portals of death? If not, then it was possible for him to join the souls of the human race. Had he really been dead all this time? If so, he knew what to expect in case he really destroyed his own brain. Oblivion!

Again the intense feeling of loneliness surged over him and held him within its melancholy grasp. Desperately, he decided to find the nearest cliff and jump from it—head-first! Humanity called; no man lived to companion him. His four metal limbs carried him swiftly to the summit of a nearby precipice. Why not gamble on the hereafter? 25X-987, understanding his trend of thought, did not attempt to restrain him. Instead, the machine man of Zor waited patiently.

As Professor Jameson stood there meditating upon the jump which would hurl him now into a new plane of existence—or into oblivion, the thought transference of 25X-987 reached him. It was laden with the wisdom born of many planets and thousands of centuries' experience.

"Why jump?" asked the machine man. "The dying world holds your imagination within a morbid clutch. It is all a matter of mental condition. Free your mind of this fascinating influence and come with us to visit other worlds, many of them are both beautiful and new. You will then feel a great difference.

"Will you come?"

The professor considered for a moment as he resisted the impulse to dive off the declivity to the enticing rocks far below. An inspiration seized him. Backing away from the edge of the cliff, he joined 25X-987 once more.

"I shall come," he stated.

He would become an immortal after all and join the Zoromes in their never-ending adventures from world to world. They hastened to the space ship to escape the depressing, dreary influence of the dying world, which had nearly driven Professor Jameson to take the fatal leap to oblivion.

1931

Joshua Glenn, who was the first to describe the years 1900–1935 as science fiction's "Radium Age," has helped popularize stories from the era for over a decade now. A former *Boston Globe* staffer and publisher of the indie intellectual journal *Hermenaut*, he is coauthor of *The Idler's Glossary* (2008), *Significant Objects* (2012), and the family activities guide *UNBORED* (2012). He is also cofounder of the brand consultancy Semiovox; and he publishes the blog *HiLobrow*.

Arthur Conan Doyle (1859–1930) was a Scottish physician and author best known today as creator of the detective Sherlock Holmes, about whom he would write four novels and dozens of short stories. He also penned historical novels, including *The White Company* (1891), and short stories including a series about Brigadier Gerard. His Professor Challenger proto-sf adventures include *The Lost World* (1912), *The Poison Belt* (1913), and *The Land of Mist* (1926).

W. E. B. Du Bois (1868–1963) was an American sociologist, historian, civil rights activist, and public intellectual. He cofounded the National Association for the Advancement of Colored People (NAACP) in 1909 and edited *The Crisis*, its magazine, for twenty years. His 1903 collection of essays, *The Souls of Black Folk*, is a landmark of African American literature. He wrote several novels and literary works, including "The Comet" (1920).

E. M. Forster (1879–1970) was an English author best known for *A Room with a View* (1908), *Howards End* (1910), and *A Passage to India* (1924), the latter two of which explore the irreconcilability of class differences. Although his 1911 collection *The Celestial Omnibus* contains several fantasy stories, Forster's importance to science fiction lies entirely in his 1909 novella "The Machine Stops"—which was a key influence on the 2008 Pixar movie *WALL•E*.

William Hope Hodgson (1877–1918) was an English poet, sailor, bodybuilder, and author of horror, fantastic, and proto-sf novels including *The Boats of the "Glen Carrig"* (1907), *The House on the Borderland* (1908), *The Ghost Pirates* (1909), and *The Night Land* (1912). He also wrote many stories, including the Sargasso Sea series, the Captain

Gault series, and a series about Carnacki the Ghost Finder—one of the very first true "occult detectives" in fiction.

Rokeya Sakhawat Hossain (ca. 1880–1932), commonly known as Begum Rokeya, was a Bengali feminist thinker, writer, educator, and political activist from what today is Bangladesh. A pioneer of women's liberation in South Asia, her major works include the two-volume essay collection *Matichur* (1904 and 1922), "Sultana's Dream" (1908), *Padmarag* (1924), and *Abarodhbasini* (1931). To commemorate her legacy, Bangladesh observes Rokeya Day every December 9.

Neil R. Jones (1909–1988) wrote over thirty Professor Jameson stories, beginning in 1931, for pulp sf magazines including *Amazing Stories*, *Astonishing Stories*, and *Super Science Stories*. He was inspired by H. G. Wells's Martian invaders, from *The War of the Worlds*, to invent the Zoromes—whose fragile brains are encased in fearsome machines. Jones's 1930 story "The Death's Head Meteor" is thought to be the first to use the word "astronaut" in fiction.

Jack London (1876–1916) was an American author, journalist, and social activist passionate about unionization, worker's rights, socialism, and eugenics. He is best known today for his novels *The Call of the Wild* (1903) and *White Fang* (1906), both of which are set in the Klondike Gold Rush, as well as for *The Sea-Wolf* (1904) and *Martin Eden* (1909). His proto-sf writings include *The Iron Heel* (1908), *The Scarlet Plague* (1912), and *The Star Rover* (1914).